THE OPERATOR

BY

DONALD E. WESTLAKE

BLACKBIRD BOOKS
NEW YORK • LOS ANGELES

A Blackbird Classic, February 2023

Manufactured in the United States of America.

Cover illustration by Mort Engle

Cataloging-in-Publication Data

Westlake, Donald E.
The operator / Donald E. Westlake.
p. cm.
1. Corruption—Fiction. 2. Private investigators—
Fiction. 3. New York (State)—Fiction. I. Title.
PS3573.E9 O64 2023 813′.54—dc23 2021938118

Blackbird Books
www.bbirdbooks.com
email us at editor@bbirdbooks.com

ISBN 978-1-61053-050-7

First Blackbird Edition

10 9 8 7 6 5 4 3 2 1

To Lee and Nedra

1

IT WAS one-thirty in the morning. I'd left Cathy's a little after one, and now I was sitting at the counter in the New Electric Diner, eating a ham sandwich and talking with Al, the night apron-man. The door behind me opened and closed, and this heavy-set type walked in and took the stool to my right. "You may not believe this," he told Al, "but I'm looking for a guy named Smith."

"If I got a choice," Al told him, "I pass."

"Unusual moniker," I said.

He glanced at me. He was fortyish, ex-middleweight, slightly seedy, stocky, big-nosed and heavy-browed. His suit was brown and old and a little too big for him. His tie was hand-painted and too wide. "It is that," he agreed. "I figure that'll help."

"What's this Smith's front name?" I asked him.

"Tim."

"Then this is your lucky night."

He slid off the stool. "You him?"

"Generally."

He started patting pockets. "A guy sent me to see you," he said. "Said you were the only private eye in this town." He frowned, still patting pockets. "Gave me a letter—" He finally patted his chest, and looked relieved. "Here it is," he said, and reached in under his lapel. His eyes got a little brighter.

I gave him a dime's worth of black coffee in the face and dove for the tile. He shot the ham sandwich and hollered, then I came back up from the floor and took the gun away from him. I may be chunky, but I can move fast when I have to.

Al was already at the pay phone, dialing Police Headquarters. I stepped back out of reach and studied the gun I was holding. It was a stubby .32 revolver, the best thing for close-up targets. Like me.

The guy who'd been packing it was wiping coffee off his face with his tie and looking annoyed.

"That's a hell of a way to start a conversation," I told him.

"If I'd known you were tipped—" He shrugged, disgusted.

"You did it yourself," I said. "You forgot not to concentrate. What's your regular line?"

"Shove it," he told me.

"I'm not all hick," I told him. "I learned some things in the Big War."

Al came back down the counter. "A car's on the way," he said. He prodded the mess of ham sandwich and splintered plate. "You could of at least waited till you got outside," he complained.

"I don't see what you called the cops for," the guy said.

That stopped me for a second, and then I said, "I thought that was kind of obvious."

"Why? I come in here to sell you that gun, if you wanted to buy it. You spilled your coffee on me while I was holding it, and it went off, accidental. No harm done. I'll pay for the plate."

"There's a gouge in the formica," Al said. He was disgusted, too.

"Okay. So I'll pay for the plate and the gouge in the formica. And for the lousy sandwich. What do we need with cops?"

"Even under normal circumstances," I told him, "that story of yours wouldn't rate much more than a horse laugh. And these aren't normal circumstances."

"Why not?"

"They told you who I was."

He shrugged. "Yeah. A private nose."

"The only private nose in town," I told him. "The only one in Winston. Do you know why I'm the only private nose in Winston?"

He shrugged again. He couldn't care less. "A hicksville like this," he said. "It couldn't support two."

"I know everybody in town," I told him. "The politicians and the businessmen and the cops. That's why

I'm the only private nose in town. And that's why these aren't normal circumstances. That's why that story of yours won't even rate a laugh."

"I'll take my chances," he said.

"Which chances are those?"

He gave another shrug, but he didn't say anything.

I waited until I was sure he saw exactly the position he was in. When he started chewing on his lower lip, I said, "Of course, there's always a way out."

He raised an eyebrow.

"All you have to do is tell me who sent you, and you can be long gone when the law gets here."

He looked disgusted again. "I make one mistake," he said peevishly. "That don't make me an amateur."

"Have it your own way."

He chewed the lip some more, but he didn't take my proposition. I hadn't expected he would. I thought for a minute of giving the .32 to Al and asking the questions with my hands, but I didn't have to. This guy would be spending a long, long night in the Winston City Jail. If I knew the local law, and I did, he'd be talking to a stenographer long before morning.

The squad car showed up a few minutes later, running without siren or flashing light. In a town this size, at one-thirty in the morning, there isn't enough traffic to make a red light necessary. And a siren would only get nasty letters in the paper about how the police have no respect for the sleeping habits of decent citizens.

Dan Archer and Pete Wycza got out of the squad car and came into the diner, both looking rumpled in their blue uniforms and shiny badges. Al and I told our stories, the stranger repeated the joke he'd told me, and Pete said, "That's real interesting, Mr.— What did you say your name was?"

"Smith," he said.

"You got that wrong," I told him. *"I'm* Smith."

"John Smith," he said.

"Okay, John Smith," said Pete. He held out his hand. "Let's see your wallet."

"I left it in my other pants."

Pete frowned. "Turn around, John Smith," he said, and when the stranger had followed orders, Pete frisked him, coming up with nothing but a key to one of the lockers down at the Greyhound station. "You travel light, John Smith," he said.

John Smith shrugged. "You got a better way?" he asked, with what seemed like genuine interest.

"Okay," said Pete. "Let's go on down to headquarters."

Pete went out the door first, with John Smith second and Dan bringing up the rear. Pete went out, stepped to the left, and waited for Smith. For just a second, Smith was framed against the door. Then the rifle boomed from across the street, and he thunked back inside like he'd been yanked.

I hit the deck again, while Dan jumped over Smith's body and through the doorway, ducking to the right and shouting, "Pete, did you see the flash?"

"No, dammit," shouted Pete.

Everything stopped for a long minute, then. Al was on the floor behind the counter, I was on the floor in front of the counter, and Pete and Dan were on the sidewalk to either side of the doorway. But nothing more happened, and when Dan moved cautiously back inside, there weren't any more shots.

Pete followed him in and shut the door. While he headed for the pay phone, Dan said to me, "What the hell is this all about, Tim?"

"You've got me," I said. "I was sitting here minding my own business, when the late unlamented over there came in and pulled a gun on me."

"You know him from somewhere?"

"Not me. He gave me to know he'd been hired."

"By who?"

"He didn't give me to know that much."

"What've you been up to lately?"

"Same old thing. Graft and corruption."

"You don't have any ideas on this at all?"

"Not a one, Dan. I'm as surprised as you are. And a bit more worried."

Pete came back then. "Ambulance is on the way," he said. To me, he said, "Tim, maybe you ought to go on down to headquarters in the morning and talk to Harcum. He'll want to know what the score is."

"So will I. Can I go now?"

"I don't see why not. Be careful going out the door."

I was careful. I pushed the door open, waited a second, and then jumped for the darkness beyond the lighted doorway. No shots. I crouched low, feeling fatter than my hundred and ninety pounds, taller than my five-foot-ten, and older than my thirty-nine years, and ran for my car, a black '51 Ford. And still there weren't any shots. Once in the car, I jammed the key into the ignition, hit the starter and the accelerator, and got the hell out of there. And still there weren't any shots.

I got about halfway home before I realized that those four big empty rooms weren't what I needed right now. What I needed was somebody to talk to, somebody to pace back and forth in front of, somebody to whom I could say, "Look, I'm still alive." Everything had whipped by at 78 r.p.m. back at the diner, and I was just beginning to catch on to what had happened. Somebody had tried to kill me. And I was still alive.

I made a fast U-turn and headed for Cathy's place. This was no time to be alone.

2

CATHY EVANS is thirty-two, seven years younger than me. She's tall and brown-haired and firmly built, and she's good-looking in a level-eyed and practical sort of way. She's Mayor Wanamaker's secretary, and she and I have had a kind of arrangement for about six years. Neither one of us is particularly anxious to stop being single, and we've never tried to kid each other about being in love and this is a deathless romance and all that jazz, and we have an arrangement that's friendly and unstrained and strictly casual.

Cathy lived in a little one-story house down on Troy Street. It was nearly two o'clock when I got there, and the windows were all dark. Tomorrow was Wednesday, a working day, so she'd be asleep by now. I pulled into the driveway, shut off the engine and lights, and crunched across the front lawn and up the stoop to the door. It was too late to use my key, even though Cathy didn't scare easy. I had to ring the bell three times before I saw a light go on. I waited, and after a minute the curtain in the front window moved and I saw Cathy looking out at me, her expression sleepy and bewildered. She blinked at me and then came and opened the door. She was clutching her blue robe closed with one hand, and her first words were, "Tim, it's after two o'clock."

"I know," I said.

"Well—" She looked beyond me, at the street, as though the answer to my oddball behavior was out there somewhere, and then she said, "Well, what is it? What do you want?"

"I'm still alive," I told her. She looked more bewildered than ever, so I said, "I want to talk. Let me in, I'll explain the whole thing."

"I've got to get up in the morning," she said. She turned away, scuffing in the slippers I'd bought her last Christmas, and led the way into the living room. I followed, closing the front door behind me.

In the living room, she said, "You want some coffee or something?"

"Something stronger than coffee," I said.

"All I've got is beer. Come on out to the kitchen."

We went out to the kitchen, and I told her what had happened, while she opened a bottle of beer and made herself a cup of instant coffee. She kept interrupting me all the way through the story, asking questions I didn't know the answers to, and when I was finished, she sat at the kitchen table, fully awake now and looking at me with round eyes. "You could have been killed," she said.

I nodded. "I've been telling you. That's why I came over here. I had to talk, I had to look at somebody and tell them I was still alive."

All of a sudden, she was crying. She didn't cover her face with her hands or anything, she didn't move, she just sat there with her hands on the table and cried, her mouth and eyes all twisted up, the tears running down her cheeks.

"Hey!" I said. I got up and ran around the table to her and put one arm around her shoulders. "Hey, cut that out. I'm still here, I'm still alive."

"You clown, Tim Smith," she said, still crying. "You clown, you clown, you clown."

"It's all over, Cathy. He's dead and I'm alive and it's all over."

"It is *not* all over." She turned suddenly, wrapping her arms around me and pulling me against her. She kept shaking her head and crying and gasping, "You clown, you clown, you clown."

"Take it easy, Cathy," I whispered. "Take it easy."

Slowly she calmed, and when finally she pushed me away and held me at arm's length I could see her struggling to keep from losing control again. "Tim," she said, "I can take my vacation anytime I want it. I can call in the morning, start my vacation right away. We can go away together. Three weeks."

"I'm not going anywhere, Cathy," I said.

"He'll try again, Tim, he will."

"No!" I pulled away from her, crossed the kitchen. "This is my town," I said. "I'm not going to run away." I turned back, glaring at her, angry now and not sure why. "Why should I run away? This is my town, goddam it. This is my home."

"He'll kill you."

"And the hell he will, too."

"We can go away for a while, Tim," she said. "Let the police work on it. They'll find out who's behind this—"

"How will they? Why do you think the bastard killed that gunman?" The madder I got, the more nervous I got, I couldn't just stand there like that, I had to do something. I had to move, go somewhere, be in motion. "I'll see you later," I said, and started toward the front of the house.

She was up and after me right away. "Where are you going?"

"I don't know. For a drive. I can't stay still."

"I'll come with you. Just let me put on some clothes."

"You go to bed," I told her. "I'll see you in the morning."

"Wait for me, Tim." She wasn't asking. So I waited, fidgeting in the living room, while she dressed. It took only a minute, but it felt a lot longer. Then she came back, wearing sweater and slacks and loafers, and we went out to the car.

Driving a car is a good way to work off steam, at least for me. We drove in silence for a while, as I glared out at the street, cutting hard into the corners and mashing the accelerator to the floor on the hills. After a few minutes, I started to talk.

"It's somebody I know," I said. "It's a *friend* of mine. A local boy like me."

"You don't know a thing about him, Tim," she said.

"I know a little. I know he has money, for instance. Hired guns from out of town—from New York, probably—don't come cheap. And I know he's influential locally, or at least he thinks he is."

"How do you know that?"

"The gunman," I said. "He wasn't worried. Thirty seconds after he'd blown the job he'd come up with the phoniest cover story in history. But he wasn't worried. Which means he was counting on more than that phony story to clear him. The only thing that figures is local influence."

"All right," she said.

"I know everybody in this town who has two dimes to rub together," I said. "They're all my friends." I made a sharp left turn, accelerating all the way, feeling the car fighting me, hearing the rear tires squeal. "My friends," I repeated. "The bastards."

We were up on the North Side, by now, Jack Wycza's territory. The town of Winston, New York, lies backed against the western edge of a spur of the Adirondacks, with a lot of hilly undeveloped forest land to the east and north. The North Side of town is all up and down.

We passed the North Winston High School, and I slowed, pointing. "You see that goddam school?"

"Yes?"

"You know what kind of cement's in that goddam school?"

She shook her head.

"*Good* cement," I said. "Because of me. Because I was nosing around and I found out they were building the goddam place with sand and I raised a bitch."

"I don't understand, Tim," she said.

"This is my town," I said. "Mine. I don't run away from it, nobody chases me out."

"All right," she said. "All right."

"In the morning, I go talk to those goddam friends of mine. There isn't a one of them I couldn't crucify and they know it. Vacation! The hell I'll take a vacation."

"I just don't want you to get killed, Tim," she said softly.

"You don't have a thing to worry about," I told her. "Not a goddam thing."

We drove in silence back to her place. I braked to a stop at the curb, and she said, "Pull into the driveway."

I nodded at the dashboard clock. "You'll only get a few hours sleep as it is."

"You're still alive, Tim," she said. "Think about that."

I thought about it. Then I pulled the car into the driveway.

3

I WOKE at ten, with sun in my eyes. There was a note from Cathy on the kitchen table, telling me to make my own breakfast, to come on over for dinner around six, and to try to keep from getting myself killed. I washed and shaved and dressed, made myself a quick breakfast of toast and instant coffee, and left the house to go find out who was rocking the boat.

I headed for my own office first, in the Western National Bank Building. I left the Ford in the bank parking lot and took the elevator up to the fourth floor. Jack, the pilot, said, "Hear somebody was gunning for you, Mr. Smith."

"It was a case of mistaken identity," I told him. "The guy actually wanted a fella name of Jones."

He gave me an employee laugh and opened the doors. I went down the hall and stopped off at Ron Lascow's office to see if there'd been any phone messages for me. I don't spend much of my time in the office, so the phone company hooked up an arrangement whereby Ron's secretary, Jess, can take my calls when I'm not around. Ron Lascow is either the town's sharpest young lawyer or youngest sharp lawyer, and we find our businesses overlap every once in a while.

"Got two," Jess told me as I stuck my head into the office. She'll marry Ron one of these days, maybe when he makes her pregnant, and it'll be a pity. She's the best-looking girl this town has ever produced, tall and slender, built like a fashion model, with long reddish-brown hair and level Lauren Bacall eyes.

"Got to what?" I asked her, as usual.

"Got to get back to my own work," she said, as usual. She handed me the two slips. "Will you be staying in the office now?"

"For a few minutes anyway."

"Okay." She thumbed the toggle that switched my calls back to my phone. I tossed her a salute and strolled over to my own place, directly across the hall.

It takes me a while to get into my office. I'm on the direct-wire burglar alarm, the one that sounds off down at Police Headquarters should anybody try to break in, and I have to clear that before opening the door. First, there's the key to open the metal box attached to the wall beside the door. Then there's the key to switch off the alarm control inside the box. And finally there's the key to the door.

I played with all these keys for a while, and finally got into my one-room office, the door closed behind me. My office is strictly functional. Having a monopoly in town, I don't have to impress my customers. So the floor is black linoleum, uncarpeted, the walls are neutral gray, the two windows overlooking De Witt Street are covered by Venetian blinds but not by curtains or drapes, and the desk and chairs are good workable office furniture, squarish and plain.

The filing cabinet is the one exception. It's one of the most expensive cabinets on the market, made of solid steel, reinforced, with a double combination lock, and it's the reason for the burglar alarm on the door. In that cabinet is everything that's happened in Winston in the last fifteen years that could have gone to court and didn't.

I sat down behind my desk and looked at the two slips Jess had given me. One was from Marvin Reed, the only son of Jordan Reed, who was the first half of Reed & King Chemicals and currently chairman of the board. Marvin, the son, wasn't doing much of anything and never had, though he was now about thirty-two. He was married, and was sitting around the old man's mansion waiting for the old man to die so he could take over the company. The "old man," though, was a hearty fifty-five, so it looked as though Marvin's taking control of the plant might occur around the same time he became eligible for Social Security.

Nevertheless, my first call was to Marvin, at home, and his wife Alisan answered. "Tim Smith, Mrs. Reed," I said. "Your husband left a message for me to call him."

"Here?"

"Yes, ma'am. Isn't he there?"

Her voice was cold as ice. "Just one moment."

I waited, just one moment, and Marvin came on the line. "I want to get together with you, Tim," he said. "Lunch all right?"

"What's the subject matter, Marv?"

"I'd rather tell you there."

"If it's something to do with Alisan, you made a mistake having me call you at home."

"It isn't anything like that," he said quickly, and added, "Though *she* probably thinks so. Hotel Winston for lunch?"

"All right," I said. I looked at my watch. "How about one o'clock?"

"Fine. I'll see you in the lobby."

"Right," I said. "So long." I held the phone to my ear and heard a click as Marvin hung up, and right after that another click. The advantages of the extension phone.

Though Alisan did have a legitimate reason to be suspicious. Marvin had decided, about five years ago, that he no longer liked the sleek slender civilized kind of woman anymore, the Alisan kind of woman. What he liked now was the blond busty come-and-get-it kind of woman. But he had his old man to worry about. Papa Reed was a bug on family. If Marvin didn't prove himself a son worthy of the Reed name, he wouldn't be getting the Reed & King plant.

So the sallies with the blondes had to be sporadic, and at a distance, usually New York. And if Marvin Reed wanted to shed Alisan—as he did—it would have to be because Alisan had failed and was no longer worthy, not because Marvin wanted freedom to cat around.

In a pretty useless bid for freedom, four years ago, Marvin had tried to hire me to tail Alisan, on the off-chance she was doing something she shouldn't. I knew the job was useless, and I don't like shadow work anyway, so I cleared the thing with the local law and let Marvin import an investigator from New York. The import had tailed Alisan until he realized nothing was ever going to happen, and then he spent most of his time boozing, with me and other locals, telling tall tales about life in the big city.

In the meantime, Alisan had caught on. Life for Marvin had not been all joy and fa-la-la for the last few years.

Wondering what silly idea was irritating him this time, I made a note about lunch on the phone slip, put it in my pocket, and looked again at the other one. Paul Masetti, it said, a name I'd never heard before. He'd called at ten o'clock and wanted me to get in touch with him at the Winston Hotel.

I phoned the hotel, and there he was. "I just got here from Albany," he said. "I may have a job for you. I'd like to talk it over with you." His voice was rough and harsh, like a back-country preacher after a long day.

"What kind of job?" I asked him.

"Have you ever heard of the Citizens for Clean Government?"

I had to admit I hadn't.

"It would be a lot easier to explain in person," he said. "If you'd have time to join me for lunch—"

"Depends on how long it'll take, Mr. Masetti. I've got another appointment at one. If we could get together at twelve—"

"Twelve is fine. Lunch, or not?"

"Better make it the bar. Lunch is what I'm supposed to eat at one."

He laughed politely and said, "I'll see you then."

I hung up, trying to figure out what that was all about, made a notation on the telephone slip, put it in my pocket with the other one, and locked myself out of my office. I crossed the hall and said to Jess, "Is Clarence Darrow free?"

"Sure," she said. "He's just counting his money."

"Again?" I went on through to Ron's office. He was sitting at his desk, frowning at the law book open in front of him.

Ron was the new-look bright young man, complete with brush-cut blond hair, black horn-rim glasses, square face, strong jawline and small straight nose. Not yet thirty, he'd been back in town from law school for five years. In that time, with a combination of smiling friendliness and legal shrewdness, he'd made a good solid place for himself in the local hierarchy.

The bottom of his ambition was the state legislature. There wasn't any top.

Now he looked up at me, grinning, and said, "People versus Smith. Baby rape."

"You get all the interesting cases," I told him. "Ever hear of the Citizens for Clean Government?"

"That's the outfit from Albany, isn't it?"

"I'm asking you."

"If it's the outfit I'm thinking of," he said, "I have heard of them, yes."

"What about them?"

He shrugged. "Reformers. Hell on wheels, gonna root out graft, corruption, kickbacks, bribery, nepotism and ass-pinching in high places."

"Is that possible?"

"You know what I mean." He closed the law book with an air of relief, and said, "They've been making a name for themselves around the state. They work out of Albany, but they're mainly hitting the smaller towns. Like Monequois and New Hamburg. Remember reading about them in the papers?"

"I haven't read a paper since Dewey was elected President," I told him.

"Well," he said, "they started with Monequois, if I remember right. That's up near the Canadian border some place. They went in there, nosed around for a month or two, dragged a truckload of evidence to the grand jury, and *kaboom!*"

"Was ist das—*kaboom?*"

"Monequois," he said, "now has a new mayor, a new police chief, two less lawyers and a saintly expression."

"They sound effective," I said.

"They are." He studied me for a minute, chewing on his thumbnail, and then said, "I was supposed to keep quiet about this, but the hell with it."

"The hell with what?"

"I take it Masetti called you, too."

"He called you?"

"Around ten. Wants me to have a chat with him at one o'clock."

"I'm on tap at twelve," I told him. "What does he want, do you know?"

"I can guess," he said. "Good old Winston is next on the list."

"I got that part of it," I said. "But what does he want to talk to us for?"

He shrugged. "I suppose he wants us to finger our friends. Reformers are like that. No sense of loyalty."

"Somebody tried to gun me last night, you know."

He nodded. "I heard about it."

"I'll bet you eighty-five cents it had something to do with this reform outfit."

"Sure," he said. "Somebody afraid to get fingered."

"The bastard."

"Who've you got dirt on, Timmy me boy?"

"Everybody," I told him. "The whole lousy crew."

"Even little me?"

I grinned at him. "As soon as that Hillview tax shuffle you worked up sneaks through the Council, yes."

He blinked. "Where the hell did you hear about that?"

"My spies," I told him, "are everywhere. Listen, Ron, what say we join forces and go see Masetti together? You free at twelve o'clock?"

"I could be," he said. "But what if I decide to sell out? I won't be able to do it with you there as witness."

"Neither will I, tax man," I said.

He grinned. "I get the point. I'll see you at the hotel at twelve."

"Fine." I looked at my watch. "I'll see you," I said. "I got business."

"Business?"

"I'm on my way to deliver an ultimatum."

"If you don't show up at twelve," he said, "I'll see if I can raise bail money for you."

4

I LEFT the bank building and walked down DeWitt Street to State, and catty-corner across DeWitt toward City Hall. Gar Wycza, in police uniform, was standing in the middle of the intersection, making believe he was directing traffic. He was one of the million or so Wyczas on the town payroll. Jack Wycza, the boss of the clan, was Councilman from the Fourth Ward, up in Hunkytown on the North Side. I waved to Gar, and vice versa, and I went on toward City Hall.

Winston was a small town, with a small town's politics and a small town's outlook. The war population boom, because of the Amalgamated Machine Parts Corporation over on Wheeler Street and the Reed & King Chemical Supplies Corporation down on Front Street, had boosted the town to upward of forty thousand people, but it still felt and acted like a town of fifteen thousand.

Now I walked through the block-square City Hall Park in the late June sunshine. A few bums were loafing on the benches by the trees, resting up between elections. Over to the left, the town library was doing a thriving business in high school students boning up for their exams. This year, the teen-agers were all imitating Sal Mineo and Brigitte Bardot, and they all looked as though they were going to do something obscene any minute.

I went through the revolving door and clacked across the marble flooring to the ancient elevator. To the ancient elevator operator, I said, "Three."

"Righteeo," he said. He pushed the gate closed, and the elevator wheezed upward. He looked at me and said, "Heerd ye had some trouble last night."

"A little," I said.

"They don't have gunplay no more like they used to," he said. "Times we had seven, eight of 'em, laying out on the City Hall lawn, dead as mackerels."

"City Hall lawn?" It seemed like a hell of a place for a gunfight, all things considered.

"Sure," he said. "That was during old Jock Shaughnessy's administration, rest his soul. When he was Mayor. Had a whiskey plant right down in the cellar, he did. Right here in City Hall." He cackled a bit at the memory.

"A whiskey plant? You mean they made the stuff here?"

"Heck, no," he said. "A *still* is where you make it. A *plant* is where you store it. Like a warehouse. Old

Flynn's gang tried to raid the plant here one night, steal the whiskey. Oh, that was a lovely fight!" He shook his head, cackling again. "They don't have gunplay no more like they did in them days," he said.

"Yeah," I said. "These are pale times, I guess."

"You betcha."

We stopped, and it was the third floor. I turned right and walked down the long corridor to the door at the end marked "Mayor Wanamaker."

Cathy was typing at her desk in the outer office. She smiled at me when I went in, and said, "What time did you get up?"

"Around ten."

"Have you found out anything about—last night?"

"I'm not sure," I said. "I'll know better by this afternoon."

"There's something funny going on around here, Tim," she said.

"Like what?"

"Wanamaker's been on the phone practically all morning, calling all kinds of people. And he had me clear the large conference room for him for three o'clock."

I nodded. "Council of war. Good. That'll save a lot of footwork. Tell him I'm here, will you?"

"Does it have anything to do with what happened last night, Tim?"

"The council of war? Probably. I'm not sure yet."

"You can tell me about it tonight. You *are* coming over for dinner, aren't you?"

"Six o'clock," I said. "I'll do my best."

"We'll have steak. And salad." She got to her feet. "I'll be right back."

I watched her walk into the inner office. Last night had been one of the few times I'd ever seen her lose control, let her emotions run away with her. And now she was back to normal again, talking about steaks and salads instead of about running away. If I were ever to get married, which was doubtful, Cathy Evans would be the woman.

She came back a minute later, held the door open, and said, "His Honor will see you now." She winked at me.

"Golly," I said. I patted her hip on the way by, and went on into the inner office, a huge, high-ceilinged, dark mahogany square, and behind the magnificent desk sat His Honor, Mayor Daniel Wanamaker, a paunchy type with a jolly baby-kissing face like a shaven Santa Claus and a pair of wire-framed spectacles that glinted in the light. He'd been Mayor of Winston for the last fourteen years, and theoretically he was local head of the Party in Power. But it was only theoretically. He was a figurehead for Jordan Reed, and he knew it as well as anybody.

"Ah, there, Tim," he said jovially as I came in, but the joviality was a little more forced than usual. Behind the big smile and the glinting spectacles, Dan Wanamaker was a worried man. "I hear you got into a ruckus last night," he said.

"That's what I'm here about."

"Here? You should be talking to Harcum, Tim. After all, *he's* the Chief of Police."

"Sure. I understand you've got a meeting set for three o'clock."

He managed to frown and still keep smiling at the same time, something only politicians can do. "Cathy shouldn't tell you my little secrets, Tim," he said.

"It's no secret," I told him. "The Citizens for Clean Government are riding into town playing Grant, and we're supposed to play Richmond. I know about that. I also know that was the cause of the *ruckus* last night. Somebody's afraid I'll play with this reform outfit, and—"

"Now, Tim!" he cried, giving a pretty good imitation of shocked surprise. "You don't think anybody in Winston, anybody you know from around—"

"Let's skip that part," I said. "I do think it, and so do you."

He shook his head sadly. "Tim—"

"Look, Dan," I said, interrupting him. "When you were elected Mayor for the very first time, you put me on your staff. Right?"

He nodded emphatically. "Certainly. Four thousand dollars per annum. And you're worth every cent of it, Tim, I want you to know that."

"Why? What makes me worth it?"

He blinked. "Well—"

"I'll tell you why," I said. "Because I can be relied on to do my work and keep my mouth shut. Because, to take a handy for instance, ten years ago when you played footsie with the repaying bid—"

"Now, Tim, now, now. That was a long time ago, Tim."

"There's a lot of stuff more recent. But I want you to think about the fact that I kept my mouth shut ten years ago, and I want you to think about what that means. For the last ten years, you've been sitting behind this desk. If I hadn't kept my mouth shut, you'd have spent the last ten years sitting behind bars, and you know it."

"Tim, it's give and take," he said. "We all watch out for one another. You do me favors, I do you favors, that's the way of the world."

"Sure it is. I go along with that one hundred per cent. But what kind of a favor was that *ruckus* last night?"

He smiled and sweated, sweated and smiled. "Tim," he said, fatherly, smiling so hard I could hear his jaw creak. "Tim, I swear to you I had nothing to do with that. Why should I have you murdered, Tim? Why should I have *anybody* murdered?"

"I'm not saying it was you. I'm saying it was somebody in this town. I'm saying it was somebody who's going to be at that meeting at three o'clock."

His smile was tacked on with thumbtacks. His gaze drifted away from mine, and his chubby hands worked on the desk. "Tim," he said, "maybe you'd better come to the meeting yourself. If there's been a misunderstanding—"

"There sure as hell *has* been a misunderstanding."

"You come to the meeting, Tim," he said. He met my eye again, and redoubled the smile. "We'll straighten it out," he assured us.

"I'll be there," I said. "But first I'll see the reform boy myself. And I just may take Ron Lascow along with me."

5

HEZEKIAH HARCUM is Chief of the Winston Police Department. Hezekiah being one of those names, he's been called nothing but Harcum for the last thirty years or more, and by now he's almost forgotten that he has a front name too.

After leaving Dan Wanamaker's office, I walked back down the hall, past the elevators, and through the door marked "Chief of Police—Private—Use Other Door."

The girl still had her clothes on, but if I'd showed up five minutes later it would have been a different story. She and Harcum were on the green-leather sofa, not quite sitting and not quite lying down. She was blond, doll-faced, big-eyed, and built like a new convertible. Harcum had been in the process of putting the top down.

He saw me and jumped up, howling. "What the hell you coming through that door? You come around the other way, same as anybody else."

"Since when?" I'd known Harcum all my life. He was a big kid when I was a little kid, and a uniformed cop when I was a big kid, a plainclothes cop when I was just recently a plainclothes civilian, and chief for the last eight years. I had *always* come through the private door, and Harcum'd never had a reason for bitching about it before.

He did now. "Since right this minute," he answered me. "You get the hell out of here and come around the other way."

The hell I would. I told him to do something to himself that would have left the blonde unemployed, and he growled, "Watch your language."

The blonde oozed up from the sofa, rearranging herself, and said, "I'll see you later, honey. For lunch." She had a voice like warm banana yogurt.

"I'll pick you up at the motel," he told her, gushing and gawking all over the place. He escorted her to the private door and patted her on the fanny as she left, with the manner of a small boy being daring. Then he locked the door—which he should have done to begin with if he didn't want anybody barging in—and turned to glare at me.

"Ease off, Harcum," I said. "I've been coming in that way for years. If you wanted me to start going around the other way, you should have said so around 1946."

He thought it over, and finally shrugged. "It was a shock, Tim, that's all. I hadn't even thought about that door."

"Looked like you weren't thinking about much else at all."

He had sense enough to be embarrassed. Harcum had never been much of a ladies' man, not even in his prime. Now, at forty-seven, he was less of a prize than ever. Stocky to begin with, years of soft easy exercise-free life with the local law had left him paunchy and double-jowled and stoop-shouldered. His black hair was thinning fast, and no matter how much he combed the remainder over the bald spot the top of his head still reflected light.

Harcum had married early, a mousy little girl even less attractive than he, and gradually she had faded into the background of his life. Three years ago, she'd died—of neglect, I think—and today's blonde was the first indication that he had some sex life in him yet.

He mumbled a bit in embarrassment, now, and sat down behind his desk. "Model from New York," he said, not looking at me. "Met her when I was down there on vacation last month."

"You don't have to explain her to me," I told him. "That's a natural phenomenon. I'm here about last night."

"Yes," he said. He looked relieved at the opportunity to change the subject, and spent a couple of minutes fussing importantly through the jumble of papers on his desk. Then he looked up and said, "Tell me about this guy Tarker."

"Who?"

"Tarker," he repeated. He checked the paper he was holding, and said, "Alex Tarker. The dead man."

"The guy who tried to kill me, you mean."

"Of course that's what I mean. Tell me about him."

"Like what, for instance?"

"Where you knew him from, what he had against you—"

I shook my head. "You've got it wrong, Harcum. I never met him before last night."

He frowned, with all his chins. "You must have known him from somewhere. Or why else would he shoot at you?"

"There was nothing personal in it," I explained. "He was doing it for money."

His frown deepened, and he fastened on me a bad imitation of a gimlet eye. "Did he say so?"

"Harcum," I said impatiently, "the guy was a professional. Take my word for it. Also, I never saw him before in my life. I— Let me see that sheet you've got on him."

He hesitated, wondering if his professional dignity would be lessened by my looking at his official documents, and finally handed it over, grudgingly. "Just came off the teletype fifteen, twenty minutes ago," he said.

It was that poor-quality yellow paper they use on teletypes, and the information was typed in huge capital letters, with no punctuation marks. It said the dead man was one Alex Tarker, a minor hood with arrest records in New York and Miami and Baltimore and one or two other places—mostly for assault, with or without a deadly weapon—and a couple of convictions, both of them dating way back. His home base seemed to be New York. The New York cops knew him better than they wanted to know him, but they didn't want him for anything in particular at the moment.

Harcum interrupted my reading, saying, "Are you sure you didn't know him from the Army?"

"Marines," I corrected him. "There's a difference. And yes, I'm sure I didn't know him from the Marines. Besides, that was fifteen years ago or more. And besides that, for the fortieth time, he was a pro. He was hired, by somebody here in town—"

He shook his head violently, jowls a-waggle, and said, "I don't like that, Tim. I don't like it."

"I didn't much care for it myself."

"No one in this town would do a thing like that," he said firmly. "I've sent a request to Washington for this man's military record. If he was in the Marines with you—"

"He wasn't," I snapped. I knew what Harcum was doing, and why. He knew he didn't have a chance of finding out who had hired Tarker, so he was busily looking for an out. On the one hand, he had the successful murder of an unknown hood from downstate. Nobody in town knew this hood or cared about him one way or the other, so there'd be no squawk if he came up with nothing on that score. On the other hand, he had the attempted murder of a prominent local citizen, namely me. For that, he had Tarker. Tarker had done the attempting and was now dead. Case closed.

Harcum liked it when he could close a case without having to do much of anything. The only thing that could cause him any trouble in this mess was the finding of the guy who had hired Tarker. That would be a real problem, so he was doing his best to make believe it didn't exist.

And I was doing my best to make sure it *did* exist. "Somebody hired Tarker," I said. "The same guy who killed him."

"Why, Tim? For God's sake, why?"

"Citizens for Clean Government," I said.

He frowned some more. "You're complicating things, Tim," he said sourly.

"No, I'm not. I'm simplifying things. You don't have to send to Washington or New York or anywhere. The guy who hired Tarker is right here in town, probably somewhere in this building."

"I wouldn't go making any wild accusations if I were you, Tim," he warned me.

I shook my head and got to my feet. "You're an ostrich, Harcum," I said. "You've got a murder to solve, and you're wasting all your energy trying to make believe it isn't there."

"We're working on it," he said defensively.

"Who've you got on the case?"

"Hal Ganz. He's my best man, Tim, you know that. He went to police school in Albany and everything. I put my best man on it."

"Sure." I went over to the private door, unlocked it, pulled it open, and glanced back at him. His forehead was lined and lips pursed, and he was gloomily studying the teletype sheet. "By the way," I said, "what's that blonde's name?"

"Sherri," he said, and looked embarrassed again.

"S-h-e-r-e-e?"

He shook his head, and spelled it out for me. "She's all right," he added defiantly.

"I'm sure she is. But I've got some advice for you."

"What?"

"Have steak and raw eggs for lunch."

6

I WENT DOWNSTAIRS to Police Headquarters, which, with the town jail, takes up the full basement of City Hall, and asked for Hal Ganz, but he wasn't around. I had to get on over to the hotel anyway, so I told the desk man not to bother looking for Hal, and I strolled out, around to the front of the building, and through the park to DeWitt Street.

The Winston Hotel is in a compromise location, midway between downtown—three blocks of DeWitt Street, including the Western National Bank and City Hall Park—and the railroad station, down State Street.

I waved at Gar Wycza again, still faking traffic control at the corner of DeWitt and State, and went on down State toward the hotel.

I walked into the lobby a couple of minutes before twelve, and Ron Lascow, looking like a suit ad in *Esquire*, got up from the lobby sofa and came over. "I think I saw our man go into the bar a couple minutes ago," he said. "Intense type, carrying a briefcase."

"God bless reformers," I said. "The bad people know he's here." I filled him in on my conversation with Dan Wanamaker, finishing, "I'm going to their goddam meeting at three."

"You told Wanamaker you were going to meet Masetti today?" he asked me.

I nodded.

"And did you happen to mention my name in passing?"

"I think so," I said. "Sure, I did. I told him you and I were going to talk to Masetti."

"I somehow wish you hadn't bandied my name about like that, Uncle Timothy," he said. "If it gets around that little Ronnie is chatting with the enemy, the boys may think I'm no longer trustworthy."

"If you *tell* them you're going to talk with the enemy," I said, "you've got nothing to worry about. But if you don't tell them, and they should happen to find out later on—"

He nodded. "I learn, Uncle Timothy," he said. "You are absolutely right."

"And the Hotel Winston bar isn't the most private place in the world," I added.

"True, true," he said. "And, speaking of the bar, let's go there."

We went there. It was practically empty, a few out-of-towners—salesmen, mostly, from the look of them—draped on the bar. Only one booth was occupied, and in it sat our man. He was exactly as Ron had described him. Intense, plus briefcase. He was sharp-nosed and bushy-browed, with deep-set dark eyes and disapproval lines etched into his cheeks. He was maybe thirty-five.

Ron, being gregarious, took over right away. He marched to the booth, put a big smile on his face, stuck out his hand, and said, "Mr. Masetti?" Masetti looked up, wary and stern. "Yes?" Ron's hand was left hanging there. "I'm Ron Lascow," he said. He used the hand to point to me. "And this is Tim Smith."

"How do you do." Masetti started to smile, which would have been something to see, but he frowned instead. To Ron, he said, "I thought I was to see you at one."

"We decided to save you some time," said Ron. He slid into the booth, on the side opposite Masetti, and said, "This way, you can double up."

"I was hoping," said Masetti sourly, "to have a chance to speak to each of you in private."

"We hold no secrets from one another," Ron told him cheerfully. "Timothy and I are blood brothers."

"We have just about the same attitude toward things," I said. I slid into the booth beside Ron, and said, "I've been hearing about your organization."

This time, Masetti did smile. It was like a blast of cold air. "What have you heard?" he asked me.

"It's a reform group," I said. "A practical and efficient reform group."

"Which may be a first," said Ron.

Masetti nodded. "It is a first," he said. "We have no political ties. We cannot be bought, and we cannot be intimidated. Do you know of our record?"

"It's impressive," I admitted.

"It's frightening," said Ron candidly.

"You have guessed, I suppose," said Masetti, "that we intend to investigate Winston next."

"And you want Ron and me to help," I said.

He nodded. "I do not come unrecommended," he told me. He reached into his suit-coat pocket and brought out a batch of business-size envelopes. He leafed through them, handed one to Ron and one to me.

I looked at the envelope he'd given me. Typed on the face of it was my full name, Timothy E. Smith. That was all. The letter inside was signed Terry Samuelson. Terry was a local boy, an old friend of mine, now a criminal lawyer in New York. I'd always respected his judgment, because he was both bright and practical, a combination you don't run into too often.

The letter was short, and to the point. It said: "Dear Tim, This is to introduce Paul Masetti, a sharp guy and a nice guy. He's working with the Citizens for Clean Government, and doing a hell of a job. I know you like Winston, and I think you'll like it even better once Paul and the CCG get through with it. Help him, if you can."

I read it twice, then folded it, put it back into its envelope, and said to Masetti, "Can I keep this?"

"Of course." He gave me another of those brief, wintry smiles. "If you decide to work with us," he said, "you can bill the CCG for the call."

"Call?"

"To Terry Samuelson."

Ron said, "Just exactly what is it you want from us, Mr. Masetti?"

"In any city," Masetti told him, "no matter what its size, there will be dishonesty somewhere in its government. The local people who work in or near the government will know where this dishonesty lies. A stranger will not. If the stranger is to root out the corruption, he must have the assistance of the honest local people." He looked intensely from Ron to me and back to Ron again. "We are not interested in the whole spectrum of dishonesty," he said. "We are only interested in dishonesty in government. Take a hypothetical example: The legal closing time for taverns in Winston is one o'clock. Let us assume that there is one tavern which stays open until three o'clock. The proprietor, in order to avoid trouble with the law, pays bribes to the patrolman on that beat and to the precinct captain or chief of police or some other authority. Two crimes are being committed, one, the crime of staying open beyond the legal closing time, and two, the crime of accepting bribes. The CCG is not at all interested in the crime committed by the proprietor of the tavern. The CCG is only interested in the crime committed by the policeman."

He paused, one finger raised to let us know that he had made only a part of the point. He delivered this little lecture with icy enthusiasm. It was obvious he had memorized it, but it was also obvious that he had memorized it because he *liked* it.

"We have a definite reason for this limitation," he went on. "And if we follow our hypothetical example, you will see what that reason is. Let us now assume that the CCG has come into Winston and, with the help of honest local citizens, has rooted out all trace of corruption in government, from the mayor's office to the cop on the beat." The way he said "cop on the beat," with the slight trace of another chilly smile made it plain that he used such slang expressions only rarely, and only for definite stylistic reasons. He didn't talk, he wrote out loud.

"With corruption rooted out," he said, "the patrolman who had been accepting bribes is no longer on the police force. An *honest* patrolman has taken his place. The proprietor of the tavern now must close at one o'clock, or be arrested." He spread his hands, and smiled once more. "Do you see?" he asked us. "By ending the first crime, we have also ended the second crime." He pointed a finger at us for emphasis. "A shockingly high percentage of crime," he told us, "could never be committed without the permission, or even assistance, of the representatives of government. Wipe out governmental crime, and you have swept away a large percentage of all other crime with it."

"Dandy theory," said Ron irreverently. "Except that governmental crime keeps coming back. That new cop on the beat is liable to be just as money-hungry as the old one."

"That is the purpose of the CCG," Masetti told him. "A permanent, incorruptible, watchful guard against corruption in government at the local level. When we are finished in a particular city or town, we leave behind us an aroused and aware citizenry, determined to keep the crooks out forever."

"What exactly do you want us to do?" I asked again. I'd had more than enough of the hypothetical example.

Masetti leveled his eyes on me. "A man in your position," he said, "gradually collects information. Some of it would be more than useful in our fight against corruption in Winston."

"I see."

Ron interrupted, saying, "What do you people get out of this? Winston isn't your town, you don't intend to live here after the whole thing is finished. What's in it for you?"

"I am on salary," Masetti told him, in all seriousness. "I have been hired as a representative of the CCG. I am paid to help in the exposing of the venal. I happen to enjoy the work very much."

"What does the CCG get out of it?" I asked him. "Satisfaction," he told me. "A job well done." He nodded at Ron. "As Mr. Lascow pointed out," he said, "I will not be living in Winston after the CCG is finished here. I have no personal or financial or political ties in Winston. Nor has anyone else in the CCG organization. We are totally dispassionate."

"What do you want from me?" Ron asked him. "Your public support," Masetti answered. "The support and well-wishes of responsible local citizens, particularly those near but not connected with the local government, is one of the best assets we can have."

Apparently, Masetti and his CCG didn't know about Ron's tax scheme, a double-shuffle he'd worked out all on his own and was planning on using as an initiation fee to get a place on the City Council next election. Under the table, Ron gave my ankle a slight kick, to ask me if I'd caught the joke. I gave him a kick back, to let him know I had.

Masetti looked at each of us in turn. "Well?" he asked us. "Have I convinced you?"

"There's only one slight problem in all this," I told him. "As you said, you aren't going to be living here after this, all blows over. But I am, and so is Ron. Both of us have to live in this town. Both of us need the tolerance and cooperation of the local politicos in order to make a living. If either of us turns against the politicians today, we're liable to have a tough time surviving tomorrow."

"Winston is a nervous town," added Ron. "Tim here hasn't even said he'd help you, and already he's been shot at once."

Masetti nodded. "I heard about that," he said. "You were very lucky, Mr. Smith."

"Very fast," I corrected him.

"But I should think," he went on, "that that should simply make you want to help us all the more. These political criminals are dangerous to your life, much more than to your livelihood."

"It's a poor life *without* a livelihood," I told him.

"There hasn't been the reform group made," said Ron, "that can get *all* the crooks. If you people leave even one of them still at his desk in City Hall, and Tim and I helped you get the rest of them, that one will still make life rough for us."

"As I said before," Masetti said slowly, "I am on salary. A very good salary, I might add. Local citizens who actively and publicly assist us are also put on salary."

"Stop right there," I told him. "Let me give you the facts of life. Do you see this suit I'm wearing?"

He nodded, puzzled.

"It was tailored for me," I told him. "Ready-mades emphasize my pot." I stuck one foot out from under the booth. "Thirty-five-dollar shoes," I said. I fingered my tie. "Imported from France," I said. "Cost me eight dollars. It's one of the cheapest ties I own. The only reason I drive a car made in fifty-one is because that's the last year a sensible car was made in this country. If I wanted, I could have a new car tomorrow, and I could pay cash. I have a nice fat savings account at the Western National, and a checking account almost as fat. I have a guaranteed income, and don't have to wait for people to come to the office and hire me."

"I understand all this—" he started, but I interrupted him, saying, "You don't understand a goddam thing. Now listen to me for a minute, and this isn't any hypothetical example, this is *fact*. There's a balance in a town like this, a balance like one of those mobiles they used to show pictures of in the magazines a few years back. Everybody has a place, and everybody has a weight, and it all balances out. You find yourself a good place, and a heavy weight, and you watch yourself, you're careful not to throw the whole mobile out of balance, and you can stay. You've got position, you've got place. As long as you help to keep the mobile balanced, your position is safe. But if you start swinging around, throwing your weight around and kicking the other parts of the mobile, knocking the balance all haywire, you'll all of a sudden find yourself out on your ear. I've got a good position, with all the money I want and all the prestige I need. I've got the position, and I'm keeping it, because I'm careful about balance, I don't throw my weight around. Ron here is just beginning to build himself a position on the mobile. As long as he shows that he respects the balance, that he isn't going to be grabby or pushy, he'll be all right. Otherwise, he's out. He'll live in this town and maybe make a kind of a living defending drunks and wife-beaters, but he'll never get onto the mobile."

"Your analogy isn't accurate," said Masetti primly. "The CCG—"

"The CCG," I interrupted him, "is out to kick the mobile to pieces. And it can't, it never will. It can maybe clip some of the parts out, disrupt the balance for a while, but the mobile will still be there when it's finished. Everybody will shift around a bit, until it balances again, and the whole thing will go on the same as before."

"It's the way of the world," said Ron offhandedly.

Masetti studied me with grim disappointment. "I was given to understand," he said, "that you had a well-formed civic conscience—"

"Hold it," I said. "Hold it just a second. Do you *know* anything about this town? Aside from the fact that the politicians are crooked, do you know anything else at all?"

"I was hoping that *you*—"

"Okay, mister, I will." I held up one hand, fingers spread, and started counting off. "The people in this town," I said, "have nothing to bitch about. Not a thing. The schools are some of the best in the state, the streets are kept in good condition, there's no organized prostitution or narcotics or racketeering, taxes are low—"

"An intelligent criminal," Masetti interrupted me, "will always cover his crimes with a veneer of good works."

"That veneer," I told him, "has made this a goddam nice town to live in."

"Why Winston, anyway?" Ron asked suddenly. "Why this town?"

"Sooner or later," said Masetti, "we will have investigated every town in New York State."

"Why start here?" Ron asked him. "There's worse places than Winston."

"Thousands of them," I added.

"We didn't start here," he said. "This is the third town we've come to. We began with—"

"What about New York City?" Ron asked him.

I said, "The hell with New York City. What about Albany, the town you people are working out of? They don't even bother with the veneer in that place. The streets are all potholed—"

"In Albany," Ron interrupted me, "property assessments are made *after* elections. That's control of the voters."

"We'll get to Albany eventually," Masetti said irritably. Albany wasn't the town he wanted to talk about.

"When?" I asked him.

"I don't know what the schedule is, I do not run the CCG."

"Who does?"

"Bruce Wheatley. You may have heard of him. He—"

"Never have," I said.

"The point," said Masetti, his irritation growing, "is that we are *now* interested in Winston—"

"Which happens to be my home," I told him.

"And have you no interest in making your home a better place to live?"

"It's a fine place to live," I said. "The mobile is well balanced, the people are getting a square deal, and the whole place is quiet and pleasant. I like things just the way they are."

"Then you won't help us." A grim sadness colored those words. With them, I had just been excommunicated.

Masetti looked at Ron and said, "And you, Mr. Lascow?"

"Uncle Timothy is my mentor," said Ron flippantly. "I've learned all about life from him."

The disapproval lines in Masetti's face deepened. "Then," he said coldly, "if you'll excuse me—"

We excused him, with pleasure.

After he left, Ron and I had a beer and talked things over. That mobile I'd been yaking about was already pretty shaky. This town was too fat, too contented. It had been a long time between reformers, and the town wasn't quite sure what to do with one anymore.

Most of the pieces of the mobile would be at the meeting in City Hall at three o'clock. Ron hadn't been invited, so I told him I'd go up to his office after it was over and let him know what had happened.

"If it looks like they're going to fall apart," said Ron thoughtfully, "it might not be a bad idea to be on the side of the angels after all." He sipped meditatively at his beer. "I understand," he said, "that this CCG is pretty effective. They just might be able to tear that mobile of yours apart after all."

"Then a new one will be built," I told him.

"Sure. And who'll be on it? The people who helped kick apart the old one."

"You have a good mind, Ronald my boy," I said. "Simple but good. I'll let you know how things look at the meeting this afternoon." I glanced at my watch and it was five of one. "I've got a lunch date," I said. "I better get going."

"Me, too," he said. "Hey, listen. Will you be needing your car this afternoon?"

"Not really. Why?"

"I'm supposed to go out to Hillview, and mine is laid up with that sick carburetor again."

"Sure thing." I gave him the key, and said, "That tax deal of yours has something to do with Hillview, doesn't it?"

"Don't go rocking the mobile," he said, grinning.

He went away, and I went off to see what Marvin Reed wanted.

7

MARVIN REED is tall and well built. At thirty-two, he doesn't show a single sign of middle-aged spread, but still has the build of a college sports star. He has dark blond hair and regular features, and since his father runs Reed & King Chemical Supplies, he can afford to dress well and does. With all of this, he just misses being handsome.

The problem isn't anything physical, really. I think it's his mental outlook, his attitude toward life. He's worried, and harried, and nervous. His wife nags at him and his father has a kind of blind hope for him. As a result, he has permanent frown lines on his forehead, his eyes have a perpetually-drooping expression of puzzled pain, and his full-lipped mouth is weak and down-curved and trembling.

He was waiting in the lobby for me, fidgeting and worrying. He looked tremendously relieved when he spied me coming toward him, as though he hadn't been really sure I'd come and talk to him after all, and he bustled me immediately off to the hotel dining room for lunch.

He was in a frantic hurry, until we sat down. Then I asked him what he wanted to talk to me about, and he began to stall. "Not until we eat, Tim," he said pleadingly. "Lunch first, and then we'll talk. All right?"

I wanted to tell him no, just to see what his reaction would be, but I was afraid he'd cry, so I said all right.

We ate lunch, and since we weren't to talk about the subject that had brought us together, we wound up not talking at all. I ate mechanically, trying not to look at him, and finally the meal was over, and it was time to get to business.

But still he stalled. I waited for him to start, and he waited for me to encourage him to start. We sat there like that for a while, and finally I gave up and said, "Well?"

"It's this letter," he said, all in a rush, and jabbed into his coat. People had been doing that to me all the time lately, reaching into their coats for letters. Once the letter had turned out to be a gun, so the letter-reaching motion now made me somewhat nervous.

But what Marvin Reed came out with was a letter. He skittered it onto the table between us and sat back, fidgeting a bit, leaving the next move up to me.

I picked it up. It was addressed to Marv at his home address, and the upper left-hand corner of the envelope told me the sender was one J. Bluger, from Albany.

The letter itself was short and to the point: "Dear Marv. In a day or two, a lawyer named Paul Masetti will be calling on you, with a letter of introduction from me. He's a fire-breathing gang-buster, working with the Citizens for Clean Government, and he's out to reform that ugly little town of yours. If you can help him, do. If you can't, don't come squawking to me. I was asked to write the letter by someone I couldn't very well refuse. I leave you to your own judgment in the matter, but wanted you to be fore-warned. Let me hear from you the next time you're up this way. Jay."

I read it through, turned it over and looked at the blank back, and said, "Who is this Jay Bluger?"

"A college friend," he said. "We still keep in touch from time to time."

"Okay," I said. I put the letter back in its envelope, and slid it across the table to him. "Now what?" I asked him.

"I got that letter yesterday," he said. "I spent all last night worrying about it, wondering what I should do. This morning, Masetti called me, asked to have an appointment with me at two o'clock this afternoon." He looked at his watch, a nervous, erratic movement. "In thirty-five minutes," he said.

"And?"

"I told him I'd go." He licked his lips, reached out to the envelope, changed his mind, snatched the hand back again. He looked pleadingly at me. "What else could I do?"

I nodded. "And where do I come in?" I asked him.

He didn't know what to do with his hands. He wanted to pick the letter up, and yet he didn't want to pick the letter up. He played nervously with the salt shaker for a minute, chewing on his lower lip. Finally he said, "You know who the people are who run Winston."

"So?"

"My father's one of them," he said, not looking at me, as though relating an up-till-now hidden sin.

"Your father's the boss," I told him bluntly.

He winced. "I can't turn against my own father," he said pathetically. He spilled salt, released the shaker, brushed ineffectually for a minute. "But I can't just—just sit aside and do, do nothing," he stammered. "I—well, I've got a, a civic responsibility, I—" He faltered miserably to a stop.

"I still don't see where I come in," I told him.

He took his courage, such as it was, in both hands, and blurted it out. "I want you to take my place. I want you to see this man Masetti at two o'clock and tell him you've been hired by me to help him as much as you can. And tell him— explain to him why I can't do anything myself."

I was shaking my head before he was half-finished. "You've wasted money on my lunch, Marv," I told him. "Masetti called me, too. I just talked to him."

He looked at me, all attention. "What are you going to, do?"

"I turned him down. You can do it, too. Explain to him yourself why you can't help him."

He looked scared and pained. "I couldn't, Tim," he said. "How could I face him?"

"That's up to you," I said. I got to my feet. "I'm sorry Marv. But that's a job I've already turned down once today."

"Tim," he said pleadingly, "could you just go and tell him why I can't help? You don't have to say you'll work with him or anything. Just tell him why I have to refuse."

I thought it over. Marvin was one of those pitiful people it's practically impossible to turn down, but at the same time I didn't feel like any more conversations with friend Masetti. "I'm sorry, Marv," I said. "It's your baby."

"I don't know what to do," he said.

"You'll think of something."

I left him sitting there, and walked out to the street and turned toward DeWitt, going back to the office. It occurred to me as I walked what it was that Marv, being Marv, would think of to do about his meeting with Masetti. He'd neglect to show up. By two o'clock, when he was supposed to be saying hello to Masetti, he'd instead be safely holed up somewhere where Masetti couldn't find him with a Geiger counter, and he'd stay holed up until he was sure Masetti had the idea. That was Marv's style.

At the corner of State and DeWitt, I waved for the third time that day at Gar Wycza, and strolled along among all the women shoppers through the June sunshine, down the two blocks to the bank building. I stopped off at Sampson's Specialty Superette, the only grocery store along the downtown section of DeWitt Street, chatted with Roberta, the boss, for a couple of minutes, and got two empty boxes, that had originally held cans of tomato soup. Then I continued on to the office.

Up on the seventh floor, I stuck my head through the door of Ron Lascow's office and said to Jess, "Anybody want me?"

"Not that I can think of," she said. She looked at the cardboard boxes. "You going away?"

"No such luck. Has Ron gone off to Hillview yet?"

She nodded. "He should be back by three."

"Hokey-dokey. I'll be in the office for a little while." She flipped the toggle, giving me back my phone service, and I went across the hall to key my way into my office. Once inside, I locked the door again, then unlocked my filing cabinet and went through the files. Stuff that had anything to do with the people who were going to be at that three-o'clock meeting went into the cardboard boxes, plus information on anybody else that might, in other hands, either send somebody to jail or leave him open to be blackmailed. When I was finished, the two cartons were bulging full and the filing cabinet was almost empty.

The phone rang as I was relocking the filing cabinet. An operator asked me if I was Tim Smith and I said I was and then she said she had a call for me from Albany.

The voice that came on was tweedy, slightly British, vaguely distracted. "Bruce Wheatley, Mr. Smith," it said.

It took me a second to remember where I'd heard that name before. Paul Masetti had mentioned it. This was the head of the CCG. "I take it," I said, "that Masetti just called you."

"He told me you refused to offer him your assistance, Mr. Smith."

"That about covers it."

"I wonder," he said, "if your decision was at all influenced by Paul Masetti's, uh, personality. He isn't, heh-heh, the most *amiable* of men and—"

"I noticed that," I said. "But that wasn't what decided me. What decided me was that I don't believe this town needs much reforming, and particularly not by outsiders." "Come now, Mr. Smith," Wheatley said heartily, "surely you aren't going to tell me Winston is the best of all possible towns—"

"It does pretty well," I told him. "The last time a reform outfit got hot around here was during the war—1944. I came back and the place was a mess. The people in City Hall were one hundred per cent honest. They were also one hundred per cent stupid."

"I assure you, Mr. Smith, Paul Masetti is anything but stupid. He may not have much personal charm, but he's a brilliant man, absolutely brilliant. The work he did for us in Monequois—"

"You don't have to apologize for Masetti. I'm sure he knows his business. But I'm sure I know my business, too, and my business is helping keep this town quiet and safe and well run. And I think it's doing all right as it is."

"Is that your final word, Mr. Smith?" He sounded disappointed, like a teacher whose most promising student has suddenly announced he isn't going on to college after all.

"That's the final word," I told him.

"In case you should change your mind—"

"I won't."

"In case you should," he insisted gently. "I'd like to give you my phone number, here in Albany. You can call me here anytime." He rattled off a number, which I didn't bother to take down, and said, "I hope I'll be hearing from you, Mr. Smith."

"I doubt you will," I told him.

I hung up, and looked at the cardboard cartons full of records. The locked filing cabinet in the locked office had always been safe enough, up till now. Now, I had the feeling there ought to be a safer place.

I got the masking tape out of my desk drawer and sealed the boxes. Then I unlocked the door and carried them, puffing, across the hall to Ron Lascow's office.

Jess looked up at me in surprise. "Are you moving in?"

"Only temporarily. When Ron gets back with my car, ask him to do a favor for me, will you?"

"Put the boxes in the car?"

"Right."

"I don't suppose I should know what's in them," she said.

I shrugged. "Why not? It's just some old stuff I've had hanging around."

"Shucks," she said. "I was hoping they were full of old mysterious secrets."

"No such luck." I grinned at her and went back to the door. "I'll see you later."

"I bet you don't even *have* any old mysterious secrets," she said.

8

Down on the street, it was still June and sunny, and the women shoppers were still bustling back and forth, lugging their shopping bags with "I've been shopping at SHELDON'S" emblazoned in red letters on both sides, and the Sal Mineos and Brigitte Bardots were still milling around the library entrance. In the window of Hutchinson's Auto Dealers, somebody was putting up huge signs for the summer sale, as Fred Hutchinson got ready to unload the last of this year's model before September, when next year's cars would be showing up. Gar Wycza was still standing in the middle of the street, at the intersection of State and DeWitt, waving his arms as though he was doing something. We grinned at each other, and as I went by he said, "Good day to go drinkin, huh?"

"When's a *bad* day to go drinkin?" I asked him.

He laughed and waved his arms, and I went on across the street. The grizzle-faced old-timers were still sitting on the benches in City Hall Park, leaning back and squinting off toward 1930.

City Hall was kind of impressive, seen from head-on. There was the block-square park, with a wide gravel walk cutting right down the middle of it from DeWitt Street to the wide stone steps of City Hall. Stately old trees—maybe they were elms, maybe they weren't, I've never been much for identifying trees—were dotted here and there on both sides of the gravel walk, and the City Hall loomed high up above them, gray-black weathered marble in a combination Greco-Roman and American Colonial style, like most small-town City Halls in the northeast, the windows wide and tall and single-paned, towers awkward and out-of-place jutting up at the corners.

It was an architectural monstrosity, complete with a little bit of Dutch influence in the choppy roofline, but it was impressive anyway. It was impressive *because* it was ugly and awkward and bulky. I guess it seemed as though a building that far from being beautiful *must* be functional.

I walked down the gravel path, and something tugged at my right trouser cuff. I looked down, and there was a new rip in the cuff. I couldn't figure that out to save myself, and I looked around on the gravel for a piece of glass or something, but there wasn't anything there but gravel and my shoes.

The tree beside me went *putt*. I looked at it, and didn't see anything in particular, and for a second I thought maybe I was going crazy. I looked around at the gravel path again, and a tiny dust puff sprang up from the path about four feet from me, toward DeWitt Street.

Somebody was shooting at me! It was the middle of the afternoon, there were thousands of people around, school kids and women shoppers and old-timers, the sun was shining down, Gar Wycza was waving his arms up at the intersection, chrome-shiny cars were driving by with muted engines, and some-body was shooting at me. And my chunky frame was too good a target to miss forever.

I was behind the tree in one quick step. I looked around, and the world was still normal. There hadn't been any sound, none of these people all around me knew I'd been shot at. One or two of the old-timers glanced at me curiously when I ducked behind the tree, but that was all, and they looked away again after a second when I didn't do anything else interesting.

The shots had come from City Hall. I peered around the tree at the building, the wide blank win-dows, feeling silly. Right in the middle of all those normal people doing all those normal things, there was a stocky nut, me, peeking around a tree at City Hall.

After the first few seconds, I didn't feel scared. I felt ridiculous, I felt as though somebody had just made a fool of me. And that made me mad. I stood behind the tree, trying to figure out what to do next, and my own helplessness made me even madder.

What could I do? I couldn't shout for help, the only people in hearing distance were the old-timers on the benches. I couldn't go charging City Hall. And I couldn't stand behind that stately old tree forever, either.

I finally backed away, heading back toward DeWitt Street again. I was trying to keep the tree between me and City Hall, and at the same time I was trying not to look like a nut playing games in the middle of the park, so I had a few awkward moments before I got to DeWitt Street. And when Gar Wycza grinned at me as I crossed the street, I growled at him, and that made me feel even sillier.

The sillier I felt, the madder I got, and the madder I got, the sillier I felt, and all the way back to the office it kept spiraling up, until finally the anger blanketed the silly feeling, and I felt nothing but enraged. By the time I got to my office, impatiently working the keys, I was boiling.

There was a shallow closet beside the filing cabinet, where I kept my overcoat in the winter. Hanging on a hook in there was a shoulder holster, and in the shoulder holster there was a .32 revolver. I had a license for that revolver, but I hadn't toted it for years, not since the first novelty of owning it had worn off, back in '46. There had never been any need for it, not in a town like Winston. There was a need for it now.

The next time somebody shot at me, God damn it, I was going to be able to shoot back.

I'd put on weight since I'd bought the gun and holster, so it fit a little too snug, but I could still move with relative freedom, and I could get at the handle of the revolver without too much struggling. I felt a lot better once it was safely on. Not quite so ridiculous, and not quite so impotently angry. I put my suit coat back on, locked myself out of the office, and went off to pound on a conference table.

9

THE MEETING was already under way by the time I got there, seven worried men sitting around a long oval table beneath a haze of blue-gray smoke. Besides Dan Wanamaker and Harcum, the seven included our District Attorney, three of the five members of the City Council, and the boss of them all, Jordan Reed.

Jordan Reed had been talking when I walked into the room. He broke off what he was saying and looked up at me, his well-scrubbed face smiling. "Tim! Come in, my boy, come in! Dan tells me you have something to say to us."

Reed was sitting at one end of the table. Among the empty chairs was the one at the other end, opposite him. I moved down to that chair and stood with one hand on its back, facing Jordan Reed and looking at each of my present friends in turn. "One of you bastards," I told them, "just took a shot at me."

The faces were startled, bewildered and innocent. Reed said, "Tim, you don't mean—"

"Why don't I mean? Not ten minutes ago somebody shot at me from this building. Last night a gunman hired by one of you people tried to kill me. That's two—"

"From City Hall?" That was Harcum, looking incredulous. "Somebody shot at you from City Hall?"

"You're goddam right somebody did. And it was one of you—"

"That's ridiculous." The speaker was Myron Stoneman, Councilman from the Third Ward. "Nobody's going to fire a gun in this building, in broad daylight—"

"*I* didn't hear a shot," added George Watkins. He's our DA, a bald butterball with a quarter cigar in its head.

Then they all talked at once, all of them agreeing that nobody had heard any shots, and none of *them* would go gunning for good old Tim Smith, and all that jazz.

I let them talk for a minute, while I looked at each of them in turn, knowing that one of these seven had tried twice so far to murder me. In that minute while they all jabbered, I tried to figure out which one.

There was Jordan Reed, the boss-man of the crowd. Paunchy, dapper, well tailored, late-fiftyish, amateur genealogist, Jordan Reed owned a fine shock of graying black hair and a soft round face lined with smile wrinkles, betrayed by eyes that were dark and deep-set and humorless. He also owned Reed & King Chemical Supplies, and he *also* owned the other six men in this room.

There was Dan Wanamaker, the shaven Santa Claus with the wire-framed spectacles and the figure-head role of Mayor. Right now his whole face and body gave an expression of worry and bewilderment and growing fear. All except his mouth. That was smiling, beaming, forgotten by its owner.

There was Harcum, born Hezekiah, slope-shouldered and heavy-faced and balding, lately the Great Romancer with the well-bottled Sherri.

There was George Watkins, the beachball DA, as round and soft and bald as Silly Putty. Originally from Buffalo, he had come to Winston fifteen years ago to work in the legal department at Reed & King. He'd apparently proved his worth, since, seven years ago, he'd been made District Attorney. He was also a cul-ture-vulture, spending a lot of time in New York, where he sank money into artsy-fartsy plays that usu-ally dropped dead.

There was Claude Brice, Councilman from the First Ward, tall, well groomed, graying, distinguished-looking and very, very stupid. The First Ward is mainly upper-middle-class professional people, doc-tors and lawyers and teachers and white-collar work-ers. Such people judge intelligence almost exclusively by appearance, which is why they were being repre-sented by Claude Brice.

There was Myron Stoneman, Councilman from the Third Ward, where they also judge intelligence by appearance. But this is a working ward, lower-middle-class population, skilled and semi-skilled labor from Reed & King and the small businesses around town. Such people instinctively distrust intelligence, and dislike anybody who looks as though he might be smarter than they. Myron Stoneman, one of the shrewdest lawyers alive, looked like a reformed hood, short and chunky and balding, with heavy jowls and a big nose and clothes invariably a half-size too large. He was a natural for the Third Ward voters.

And there was Les Manners, Councilman from the Fifth Ward. His voters were middle-middle, *Time-Life-Satevepost* readers. Les looked like the prototype businessman, complete with blue or gray double-breasted suits, slate-gray hair carefully parted on the left side, and the squarish face of a ruggedly handsome man who had aged gracefully and still, at fifty-three, got up before dawn the first day of hunting season.

These were the seven, and one of them was trying damn hard to be a murderer. *Was* a murderer, of Alex Tarker, but that apparently didn't count. He wanted to be my murderer, and nobody else's.

They didn't know it yet, but their minute of jabbering was up. I opened my suit coat and pushed it back at the sides, putting my hands on my hips, so the butt of the .32 peeked around the lapel. It was a melodramatic gesture, but the hell with it. I felt like being melodramatic.

Besides, it shut them up. Into the wide-eyed silence, I said, "Twice in the last twenty-four hours, there've been attempts on my life. One of you people here—"

"Why us?" George Watkins again, pushy and demanding.

"You know why as well as I do," I told him. "The CCG."

Jordan Reed, his fleshy face beatific in a salesman's smile, said, "You're one of us, Tim, you know that."

"Of course," said Les Manners.

"No, I don't know that," I said. "I know I've cooperated with you people in the past, and you've cooperated with me—"

"Well, that's what I mean," said Reed.

"But that doesn't mean," I said, drowning him out, "that I'm on the Jordan Reed string, like the rest of this crowd."

"We're not on any string," said Myron Stoneman angrily.

"Of course not," said Les Manners indignantly.

"That isn't the question," said Reed smoothly, and I knew he damn well didn't want it to be the question.

"The question," I said, dragging them back to what I'd been talking about, "is whether or not I can feel safe in this town, as long as you people are running it. If I can—"

"Now, Tim," Reed started, placatingly, smiling at me some more, while the others all looked to him for help.

I wouldn't be interrupted. "If I can," I said again, louder, "then you people can feel safe from me. If I can't, then neither can you."

"That sounds something like a threat, Tim," said Les Manners, in his most businesslike manner.

"It is a threat," I told him. "You people know I talked to Paul Masetti of the CCG, just a couple hours ago. He asked me to work with him, to help him get the goods on all of you."

"You wouldn't do that, Tim," said Reed.

"Not if I felt safe," I told him. I looked at each of them in turn. "You people," I told them, "are safe from me only as long as I'm safe from you. But if it comes to a showdown, there isn't a one of you I wouldn't crucify."

"We've all been kind of upset, Tim," said Claude Brice, looking intelligent as hell.

"We know where we stand now," George Watkins added firmly, in the same tone he undoubtedly used when talking to the director of one of his Broadway flops just before opening night. "We can handle this CCG business," he said positively, "so there's no need for anybody to fly off the handle."

"*If* you're right," Myron Stoneman told him.

George bristled. "I'm right," he snapped.

I didn't know what they were arguing about, and I didn't care. "There've been two tries," I said, breaking into their squabble. "There better not be a third."

"There won't be a third," Reed told me soothingly.

"Of course not," piped up Dan Wanamaker, smiling at me like an ad in the *Saturday Evening Post.*

"I want to be sure of that," I insisted, ignoring Dan, talking to Reed.

Harcum piped up. "Let me get things straight now, Tim," he said, giving a passable imitation of competence. "Do you want me to look for whoever it was took the shot at you and hired Tarker, or do you just want the guy to stop gunning for you and if he does everything's forgiven and forgotten?"

"I want him to stop," I said.

He looked puzzled. "Then what about me?"

"You do whatever you want," I told him. "The guy you're looking for is one of the seven people at this table. Do you want to take a chance on booking one of these pals of yours? He'd want to make damn sure he dragged you down with him, wouldn't he? And he could do it, too, couldn't he?"

"This makes it damn tough, Tim," he said.

"Do *you* want him caught?" Les Manners asked me.

"I want him to stop," I said. "If he does, then the whole thing is over and forgotten, and we all go on the way we've done in the past. If he tries again, I turn the CCG on the whole lot of you."

"What you're saying, in effect," said Myron Stoneman softly, "is that this person shouldn't miss the next time. He should make sure he kills you."

"He'll miss," I told him. "I've seen him in action twice now. He's too clumsy. He'll miss again."

"He may improve with practice," Stoneman said.

Jordan Reed suddenly wasn't smiling. "There won't be any more practice," he snapped. "And that's that." He looked at me, serious now. "I don't know who the idiot was, Tim," he said. "But he's finished, I guarantee it."

10

ORDINARILY, Jordan Reed's guarantee is rock-solid in Winston, something you can rely on absolutely. But there was nothing ordinary about the current situation, so I did my best to shore up Reed's guarantee with some guarantees of my own.

The first thing to take care of was my ace in the hole, my files. Leaving City Hall, I went back across the park without being shot at, smiled at Gar Wycza for the thousandth time that day, and walked on down DeWitt Street to the Western National Bank Building, and beyond it to the bank parking lot. I traded hellos with Jakey, the uniform-capped old man who presides over the parking lot, and looked around to see if Ron Lascow had come back with my Ford.

He had. It was over in the corner, in its usual place, and Ron Lascow himself was emerging from the back seat, coming out rear first. I went on over, and he turned as I reached the car. "Just in time," he said. He brushed his hands together in an exaggerated gesture, and said, "I've done all your work for you,"

I looked in the window, and saw the cardboard cartons sitting on the back seat. "Thanks, Ron," I said. "I appreciate that."

"What the heck you got in those things, anyway?" he asked me. "They weigh a ton."

"Just some old out-of-date files I'm getting rid of," I told him.

One of the nice things about our office building," he said, "is the janitor service."

"I thought I ought to burn this stuff myself," I explained. "It's all old stuff, pretty useless to me, but there's no sense taking any chances with it."

He took off his horn-rims and removed perspiration from the bridge of his nose with thumb and forefinger. "I kept all the good stuff," he told me. "I knew you wouldn't mind. All about divorces and juicy stuff like that."

"Paperbacks are hotter," I suggested. I stepped around him and opened the driver's door of the car. Sitting in it, my feet hanging out the side, I looked up at him. "In case I stop being lucky," I said, "I'd like you to do me a favor."

He frowned. "What do you mean, stop being lucky?"

"If I'm killed," I said. I was doing my damnedest to think of some way to say it that wouldn't sound like dialogue from a Grade B movie.

"You mean that business last night?"

"Someday I'll tell you the whole story," I said. "In the meantime, will you do me the favor?"

Puzzled and curious, he nodded and said, "Name it."

I motioned at the cartons in the back seat. "I'll let you know where I stash this stuff," I told him. "Or, if I don't get the chance, ask old Joey Casale. You know him?"

"The grocer out your way," he said.

I nodded. "In case I'm, well, killed, I'd like you to give those cartons to Masetti."

He looked doubtful. "Well—"

"There's nothing in there on you," I assured him. "And Masetti looked to me like the kind of guy who wouldn't spread it around where he got the stuff, if you asked him not to."

"All right," he said. "But I don't expect it to happen."

"Hell, neither do I. If I did, I'd be in Florida by now."

"Is that why you wanted me to bring the cartons down?" he asked me. "So nobody would see you carrying the stuff out of the building yourself?"

"Partly," I said. "But mainly, I was beginning to worry about that waistline of yours. You haven't been getting enough exercise lately."

"If you stir things up around here, Tim," he said, "I'll get all the exercise I need."

"Every cloud has a silver lining," I told him, and slid around to face the steering wheel. "Don't take any wooden defendants," I told him.

"Hang by your thumbs," he suggested.

We nodded to each other, and I started the car and drove away, headed home.

Home, for me, is a four-room apartment on Bleecker Street, the full second floor over Casale's Grocery. I have no neighbors to speak of, which is exactly the way I like it. The building is on the corner, with a garage-and-loft next door on the other side. There's no third floor, the grocery closes at eleven, and the Casales live across the street. It's a great place for wild parties, so maybe I'll have a wild party there someday.

Now, I left the Ford in my parking space behind the building and went around front and into the grocery. Joey, the patriarch of the huge Casale family, was on duty alone, sitting on a backless kitchen chair behind the counter and reading the comics in the newspaper.

Joey Casale had arrived in the States in the classic manner, that is, with no money, no command of the English language at all, and a card with his name on it tied to a buttonhole. He'd spent his adolescence in Brooklyn, with an aunt and uncle, learned English, fought with the uncle, got married, and moved upstate to Winston. He started the grocery store and a family. The grocery store hadn't grown much, but the family had gone wild. He had four sons, each of whom had at least four kids of his own, and some of those kids were now having kids. There were Casales all over town, most of them in one kind of small business or another, from Mike Casale's trucking company to Ben Casale's laundromat.

Old Joey, at seventy-three, was still the iron-fisted patriarch. The family revolved around him, a cohesive and clannish unit. He was a short, wiry, dehydrated old man, with sharp unblinking black eyes in the middle of a lined and weathered face. I'd known him since I was a kid, and his oldest boy Mike and I were baseball buddies. He was a second father to a lot of kids of my generation, and when, after the war, I came home and, my father having died in '43, started looking around for a place to live, I was glad for a chance to rent the apartment over Casale's Grocery.

Joey put the paper down when he saw me come in, smiled, and got to his feet. "A six-pack of beer," he said, "and what else?"

"Nothing to buy this time, Joey," I told him. "I'd like you to do me a favor, if you would."

He spread his hands in an is-there-any-doubt movement, and said, "Of course I would. What do you think?"

"I've got a couple of tomato-soup cartons out in the car," I told him. "They've got stuff in them I want to stash away for a while."

"Well, sure," he said. "Don't be silly, bring them in."

"Thanks, Joey."

"Where's the car, around back?"

"Uh huh."

"Okay, I unlock the back door."

"Fine."

While he went off to remove the bolt and wiring and padlock from the back door, I went out the front

way and around to the car. I looked up and down the
street, but didn't see anybody, and then the back door
creaked open, and I carried the two cartons in, one at
a time.

Joey scuttled ahead of me, off to a far corner of the
storeroom, and said, "Here. Put them back here." I did
so, and he looked at the result clinically. "Looks good,"
he decided. "Looks all right. Two tomato-soup cartons
in a grocery store, what's wrong with that?"

"Nothing's wrong," I answered. "It looks natural."

"Sure," he said.

"If Ron Lascow ever should come looking for this
stuff," I said, "give it to him. But nobody else."

"Ron Lascow," he said, and added a few more lines
to his face by frowning. "That young lawyer kid? With
the dark rims on his glasses?"

"They all look like that," I told him. "But you've got
the right one."

"Okay," he said. "Him or you. Anybody else, I don't
know what they're talking about."

"Fine. And I guess I'll get a six-pack after all."

I got the six-pack, and went on upstairs. Joey
Casale owned the building, and my apartment had
originally come famished, with the kind of stuff you
always find in furnished apartments, but over the
years I've replaced it all with my own things, piece by
piece. Every once in a while, I'd call Joey to have a
couple of his kids move something out. The only
things left that I don't own are the refrigerator and
the stove.

The apartment, now that I've got it the way I want, is a pretty good one. From the street, you go in the door to the right of the grocery windows, up the stairs, and into what was originally supposed to be the dining room. I use that as my living room, with the usual sofa and armchairs and lamps and tables, and the walls rubber-base painted a light green. The rug is gray and wall-to-wall.

I added double doors to separate this dining room from the old living room, which I now use as a kind of den, library and office-away-from-office. There's an old desk in there, and some glass-doored bookcases, and a filing cabinet containing stuff less important than the files I'd just removed from downtown.

In the other direction from the living room, a hall leads back to the kitchen, with the bedroom on the right and the bath on the left. There used to be a back staircase, but I didn't want it much, and when Joey's kids made his storeroom larger downstairs, they'd ripped that staircase out and made the second-floor space a huge storage closet.

I went into the kitchen, opened a beer, put the rest in the refrigerator, washed hands made dusty by the soup cartons, and changed my limp shirt for a fresh one. I finished the beer, and looked at my watch. It was four-twenty, time to go.

I wanted to talk to Hal Ganz. He was the detective Harcum had put on the Tarker killing, and he was good at his job, in a limited way. He wasn't very bright, but he was strictly honest, the plodding, patient type.

And he had the facilities of the Police Department to help him.

I knew Hal went off duty at four o'clock, so he'd be on his way home now, out to Hillview. I'd go out and have a talk with him, suggest a merger. Since he was a cop, there were things he could do that I couldn't. Since he was scrupulously honest, there were things I could do that he couldn't. We ought to make a great team.

11

THE SECOND WORLD WAR caused quite a population boom in Winston, and with a population boom there comes a housing boom. The last couple of decades have seen the flowering in Winston of the ranch-style development. We have a number of them already, with another one going up every once in a while, and Hillview, where Hal Ganz lived, was the first of them.

Hillview was thrown together in '47, in time to catch the veterans and the defense workers while they still had cash in their pockets, and while the veterans in particular were all getting married and starting families and looking for a place to live. Built on a filled-in swamp just to the west of town, Hillview is as flat as a pool table, though it is possible, on very clear days, to see the hills and mountains way over on the other side of town.

The builder of Hillview was a Winston man, now living in Florida on his profits, and he scrupulously followed the ideas of every other development builder in the country. The streets were blacktop and curving and named after flowers. The houses were two- and three-bedroom brick ranch-styles, most of them without cellars or attics. There's a shopping center in the middle of it all, a school off in one corner, and a firehouse down the road toward town.

In '47, it all looked pretty fine. Nice new houses, kind of shoe-boxy but sparkling and clean, with attached garages and curving flagstone walks leading to the front doors. The people living there were mostly young, either childless or with maybe one kid of pre-school age. It was a pretty good place to live.

Hillview is now halfway through its second decade, and it hasn't aged very well at all. A lot of the original owners got out from under in the first few years, before the floors got too warped and the windows began to stick and the plumbing went haywire. And the people who moved in after them were buying second-hand houses, and not very good second-hand houses at that, so they didn't try very hard to keep them up.

And the kids began to grow, and the city and the county never did settle the argument as to which one of them had the responsibility for keeping up the streets in Hillview, so neither of them did anything, and a few of the houses were empty, and a couple of the houses were no longer safe for human occupancy.

Only a little more than a decade after it was built, Hillview was a bedraggled mess. Most of the lawns had been tromped into bare brown earth by kids playing Indian. The empty houses had had their windows broken. The blacktop streets had suffered from frost heaves after a few particularly severe winters, and were now crumbled and potholed. The whole area was littered with tricycles and wagons and hanging laundry and screaming kids and straggle-haired housewives and door-to-door salesmen. One of the empty houses, down near the shopping center, had caught fire and burned almost to the ground before any of the neighbors thought to call the Fire Department. The blackened remains, limp and soggy-looking after one winter, were still there.

As families grew, some people put on additions to their houses, and most of them knew even less about building than the original developer had. The resultant sheds and lean-tos and clapboard horrors jutted out here and there onto backyards and front lawns, and the whole development was looking more ramshackle and beat-up every day.

And, although the people of Hillview didn't know it, the worst was yet to come. If Ron Lascow's little double-shuffle got through, Hillview would have a historical right to start a second American Revolution, because they were about to get taxation without representation. And without street repair, too, which would probably bother them more.

The people who got the worst deal out of the whole thing were the vets who had paid for their nice new houses with GI mortgages. They could sell if they dared, let the new owner take over the payments, but a GI mortgage is different from any other. If the new owner misses a payment, the vet who thought he'd sold the house has to make it up. Very few vets wanted to take a chance on that, and so they stayed, no matter how lousy the neighborhood got. Most of them had twenty-year mortgages, and they planned to move in that twenty-first year. By then, they might get back a quarter of what they'd paid for their houses. If they were lucky.

Poor Hal Ganz was one of these vets. He lived deep within Hillview, where you couldn't see the faraway mountains no matter how clear the day was, and he'd be there until 1968.

You could tell the houses that still had their original Owners. Most of them had fenced-in lawns and relatively fresh coats of paint on the wood trim of their houses, and most of them had planted something in the front lawn, hedges or a row of flowers against the front wall or a rock garden.

Hal Ganz had a rock garden, and he was fooling around with it when I pulled to the curb in front of his house on Chrysanthemum Road, about twenty to five. Farther down the street, some subteen kids were playing the noisiest game of hide-and-seek ever heard.

Farther up the street, somebody was attacking his six-teenth of an acre with a power mower. A teen-age kid across the street was tinkering with the motor of a car parked in the driveway.

I got out of the Ford, which felt right at home in these surroundings, and waved at Hal. "How you doing?"

"Doing okay, Tim," he said. "What brings you way out here?"

"Wanted to talk to you," I said. I hunkered down beside him and tried to look at the rock garden as though I were interested in it. "Planting?" I asked him.

"I planted in April," he said, and then I noticed some little green things sticking up out of the dirt. "There should be more coming up than this," he said. He sounded bitter, and I had the feeling it was more than the rock garden.

Hal Ganz was a rangy, hawk-nosed, sandy-haired guy with a perpetual expression of sober bewilder-ment. A not-very-bright plodder, an honest guy, a saver and a worrier, who would always try to do well by his job and his wife and his children and his com-munity. He had a right to feel that Hillview was a pun-ishment he didn't deserve.

"Maybe they're slow this year," I said, pointing at the little green things and trying to be helpful.

"I didn't know you had a green thumb, Tim. You want some beer?"

"I'd love some beer."

I followed him through the garage and into the kitchen, where Joan Ganz was hacking an onion with a knife. We said hello to each other, Hal brought out two cans of beer and opened them, and then he and I went on into the living room and sat down.

He started the conversation. "You want something from me, Tim."

I nodded. "Some help," I said. "A pooling of interests."

"Is this about the killing last night?"

"Uh huh. The person or persons unknown who shot Tarker is or are the same person or persons unknown who hired him to shoot me." After that sentence, I took a long swig of beer. "I'm interested in that guy," I went on, "maybe even more than you are. He tried for me again this afternoon and—"

"Again?"

So I told him about the shooting in City Hall Park, and when I finished he shook his head and said, "I was afraid of that. Chief Harcum kept trying to tell me Tarker must have known you from somewhere, from the Army or something, but I was pretty sure somebody local was behind it." Hal had been sent away to the police academy in Albany, where he learned a lot of theory he seldom got a chance to try out in practice, and he'd come back to be the only person in town who called Harcum "Chief."

"It's more than somebody local," I told him. "I can narrow it down to seven people for you." And I gave him an edited story of the CCG and my little talk with the boys this afternoon.

When I finished talking, he grimaced. "Politics," he said. "I was afraid it was going to get all mixed up with politics." He took a swallow of beer and stared gloomily across the room. "I don't like politics," he said.

"There are times," I told him, "when I couldn't agree with you more."

He sighed and shook his head. "All right," he said. "It's one of the seven. Can you narrow it anymore than that?"

"Not yet," I said. "Any one of them has the money to hire a gun. And they all go off to New York for a weekend of theater every once in a while, so any one of them had the opportunity to contact Tarker."

"I suppose they all have hunting licenses," he said.

That stopped me for a second, and then I got it. "Tarker was shot with a hunting rifle?"

He nodded. "Thirty-thirty. Deer rifle."

"Deer hunting is pretty popular around here," I said.

"I know."

"I've told you all I've got," I said. "What have you got?"

"Nothing," he said. "A body and a used bullet. The New York police know Tarker, but they don't have any way of checking back on him, to find out who might have hired him. And all he had on him was a key to one of the lockers at the Greyhound depot."

"What was in the locker?"

"A suitcase. One of those small blue canvas things."

"An AWOL bag."

He nodded. "Nothing in it but clothes and his return ticket to New York. And the gun he was carrying was untraceable."

"That wouldn't have led to the guy who hired him anyway," I said. "The gun would only lead to some New York pawnshop somewhere."

"I don't know, Tim," he said. "There just isn't anywhere to go. We figured out where the killer shot from—figuring the angle the bullet went into the body—and it was the roof of that movie theater across the street from the diner. We went up there and looked around, but there wasn't a thing. Not even a used cartridge. He must have taken it with him. Sometimes, you can get a good fingerprint from the base of a cartridge. Where the guy pushes it into the gun." That part had come straight from his police academy training. "But there just wasn't anything up there," he finished.

"How did he get on top of the movie?"

"Fire escape in back. He must have come down the next block over, Morton Street. There's a short alley leading to the back of the theater, where the fire escape is. He went up that and onto the roof. There's a fake wall in the front of the theater, sticks up about five feet above the roof. So he just steadied his arm on that, and fired. Then he went back down the fire escape and drove away."

"We know how," I said, "and we know why. Now all we need is who."

He gave me a wan smile. "That's the tough part," he said. "It usually is."

"I'd like to work with you on this thing, Hal," I said. "We keep in touch, tell each other anything we find out."

"You aren't going to do something like those private detectives in books, are you? I mean, you aren't trying to catch him yourself so you can shoot him or anything?"

"Hell, no," I said. "I like my license too much for that. We find him, and you put him behind bars, and then he can't shoot at me anymore. That's all I want."

"Okay," he said. "We'll work together. But I don't know what we're going to work on. I don't have a thing."

"Something will break," I told him.

"I hope so."

"Mind if I use your phone?" I asked him.

"Go right ahead."

I called Cathy, at City Hall. I'd just remembered I was supposed to go over to her place for dinner, so I told her to hang around for a while, and I'd pick her up and drive her home. Then I thanked Hal for talking things over with me, and we assured each other something would turn up.

Driving back through the sad community of Hillview toward town, I thought again about Ron Lascow's little scheme, and I had the idea it would be a good thing if Ron came out here and looked at the people he was about to put the squeeze on. It might change his mind. I knew right now it was simply an abstraction on paper for him, something clever and intricate he'd worked out, and that he was proud of because it was clever and intricate and he had worked it out.

That's the trouble with kids like Ron. They see the beauty of a clever plan, but they never see the people. I decided that was going to have to be my good deed of the day someday soon. Bring Ron Lascow out here and rub his nose in Hillview a little. It would be good for him.

12

GEORGE WATKINS, the world's fattest DA, hailed me in the corridor at City Hall. I turned and waited, and he came puffing toward me at a half-trot, his bald head gleaming beneath the overhead globes. "You got a minute, Tim?" he panted, when he reached me.

I checked my watch. It was almost five-thirty, and Cathy was supposed to be finished work at five. "A minute," I said. "But not much more."

"This won't take long," he promised. "Come on into my office."

He led the way, going at a more sensible pace this time, and I fell in beside him. His secretary had gone from the outer office, and he led me through and inside, where he motioned me to sit down and himself settled gratefully behind his desk.

I noticed a thick sheaf of papers on his desk, bound in maroon cloth, a title stamped on the cloth in gold. "New play?" I asked him.

He nodded happily. "Got it in the mail yesterday," he said. "They want me to put some of the money up."

"Will you?"

"I think so." He patted the manuscript fondly. "Looks like a real hit to me," he said.

I leaned forward and read the title upside down. *A Sound of Distant Drums.* If it was a hit, it would be George's first. "Good luck," I said.

"Thanks." He became suddenly businesslike. "I won't beat around the bush, Tim," he said. "It's about this CCG thing."

"I'd guessed that part of it," I told him.

"Now, the CCG," he said, "is a political outfit, just like any other. Take it from me. All they want is a reputation, to be able to say they've cleaned up this town and that town and the other town. But they've got ambitions, you can count on it. I don't know what, whether they're trying for Albany or New York City or the whole state or what, but they've got a purpose behind all this."

Judging from Masetti, their purpose was pretty virginal, but I nodded anyway, to help him get to the point.

"The way I see it," he said, "they're going to be wanting friends later on. Once they've got their reputation made, and they're ready to make their move, they'll want friends. And that means," he concluded triumphantly, "that they'll make a deal."

That one caught me off guard. "A deal?"

"Of course. We make it easy for them, give them their scandal on a silver platter, and then they make it easy for us."

"That sounds like desperation talking, George," I said.

"The hell it is. Tim, look. No outfit could be as efficient and tough-minded and politically aware as the CCG and be totally clean."

"Is this what you and Myron Stoneman were arguing about at the meeting?"

"Myron," he said disgustedly, and made a brushing-away motion. "They'll make a deal, I'm sure of it."

I shrugged. "So be sure of it."

"Now here's the thing," he said. "We can't risk having an elected official seen talking with anybody from the CCG, so there's the problem of who's going to suggest the deal. We want you, Tim. You're safe. You can make the suggestion, and even if they turn it down they can't touch you. You aren't an official."

"What's the deal?" I asked him.

"You'll do it?"

I wouldn't, but I was holding back the refusal till I got the story. "First tell me what the deal is," I said.

"We give them one man," he told me. "One man to raise a stink about."

"Who?"

He looked doubtful, and hedged. "We aren't one hundred per cent sure yet, Tim." Which was a lie. They were sure, but they wanted an out in case I was loudly opposed to their choice.

"Who do you think?" I insisted.

"Jack Wycza."

Jack Wycza. City Councilman from the Fourth Ward, over in Hunkytown on the North Side, where the factory workers from Amalgamated Machine Parts all lived. His cousin Gar was the traffic cop I'd been exchanging grins with all day. His other cousin Dan was one of the cops who'd come out to the diner last night after the shooting.

The thing was, Wycza was an independent force up there in Hunkytown, free of City Hall and unpredictable. If somebody had to be thrown to the wolves, he was the natural choice. He was a Councilman, which was enough for a good-sized scandal on the local level. And he was a thorn in the side of the City Hall regulars, because he was a free agent. And, last but not least, he was kept out of the general monkeyshines, so he couldn't return the favor by hollering on anybody else.

It wouldn't be hard to nail Jack Wycza, either. Within his own ward, he'd broken almost any law you've ever heard of. Every last one of his relatives was drawing a city salary. He got pay-offs and kickbacks and protection money all over the ward. He ran his own horse-room on Miller Street. He was very, very nailable.

"What do you think, Tim?" George asked me.

"I think it stinks," I said.

"Because of Wycza? We can always get somebody else, Tim. It doesn't have to be Wycza."

So I'd been right about the hedge. "It doesn't have to be me either," I said. "The hell with Wycza. I'm not running your errands, I'm not doing your dirty work. I do this, and somebody makes a phone call to the Fourth Ward and says, 'Tim Smith was—'"

"None of us would do a thing like that," he said. He was shocked, he was.

"Hell, no. And none of you would take a shot at me either."

"Tim, look, you're one of us—"

"And the hell I am, too."

"We have to know where you stand, Tim," he said. "We have to be sure of you."

"I don't stand," I told him. "I'm out of it. This is your war, and I don't want any part of it, and I'm not going to *have* any part of it."

"I don't know, Tim—"

"Well, I know, and I'm telling you." I got to my feet. "Count me out," I said. "Fight your own battles."

I started out of the office, pausing at the door to look back at him and point at the play manuscript on his desk. "Good luck with that," I said.

He didn't answer me.

13

DURING DINNER, I told Cathy my day, in a slightly edited version. The one thing I left out was the gunfire from City Hall this afternoon. She laughed when I described Paul Masetti, and nodded with satisfaction when I told her about the meeting with the seven likely candidates, and frowned when I told her about George Watkins having asked me to finger Jack Wycza.

When I was finished, she said, "They're all scared, Tim. I've never seen so much activity around that place as there was today. Dan Wanamaker was making all kinds of phone calls, including one to that travel agent in the Winston Hotel."

"Kilmer?"

"Uh huh. And George Watkins kept running in and out all day long, both before and after the meeting."

"Trying to convince everybody he was right about the CCG," I guessed. "So they could then turn around and convince him."

"What about the man who tried to kill you?" she asked. "Don't you have any idea at all which one he is?"

I shook my head. "Not even a guess. And that's pretty disgusting when you stop to think about it. Somebody tries to kill me, and the likely prospects are seven of my closest and oldest friends, men I've known practically all of my life, men I've worked with for the last fifteen years. And I not only can't even make a guess as to which one it is, I can't *eliminate* any of them. Not a one. That's a hell of a thing to be able to say, Cathy, that I can't look at a single one of those seven people and know absolutely that he wouldn't try to kill me."

"How deeply are you involved, Tim?" she asked me suddenly.

"In what?"

"In anything that might interest this reform group."

I shrugged. "I'm not directly involved in any graft or kickbacks or nepotism or anything like that, if that's what you mean."

"But what?" she prompted.

"But I have lived here for the last fifteen years. I have worked at my job, and it's put me in contact with City Hall, and there has been a lot of mutual back-scratching. That was inevitable."

"And look at the people you got involved with that way," she said. "You just told me you couldn't look at a one of them and be sure he wouldn't try to kill you."

I frowned. "I don't see what you're getting at."

"They were the wrong people to get involved with, Tim," she said.

"I didn't have much choice," I told her.

"You could have chosen not to get involved."

"No, I couldn't. Everybody's involved, one way or another. You've got to get involved, if you're going to get anywhere in life."

"You mean," she said, "that you have to be dishonest."

That was a strong accusation, and completely unexpected, and I found myself automatically in hot defense. "I'm not dishonest," I said. "Not at all. Look, Cathy, don't confuse me with the police. Their job is to find the criminal and see that he's punished. My job is strictly investigation. I'm hired to investigate, and it's up to the people who hire me what they do with the stuff I dig up. I play ball with them, and they play ball with me, and everybody's satisfied."

"What if you don't play ball?"

I laughed. "I'd make a fast fifteen hundred a year doing credit checks."

"So you have to play ball," she said. "You have to make a deal with people like these seven."

"You're making it sound a hell of a lot worse than it is," I told her.

"People get away with things with your help," she said.

"Without my hindrance," I corrected her.

"That's the same thing."

"No, it isn't. Cathy, nobody has ever come to me and said, 'Here, Tim, here's a couple hundred. I'm getting a kickback on that street-paving job, and I'd like you to look the other way.' If I find out about the kickback, I find out afterward. And if there's no point in raising a stink, I don't raise a stink."

"They still pay you off," she said. "You get money from the city, and from Reed & King, and from Amalgamated—"

"Investigator," I said. "It's on the payrolls. And I work for the money."

"Tim," she said, her face serious and intense, "it doesn't work that way. It can't. You can't just say that your job is to have no conscience, and so people can't blame you for not having a conscience because that's your job. Either you're honest or you're dishonest. If you're faithful to the rules of your job, and your job is a dishonest one, then you're being dishonest."

"I am no more honest or dishonest than anyone else in the world," I said. I didn't particularly care for this discussion, and I wanted it to end as soon as possible.

But she wouldn't let it go. "You are," she said. "You have a greater opportunity to be one or the other."

I pushed back from the table and got to my feet. "Let's go into the living room and talk about other things," I said. "We're not going to prove anything one way or the other."

"I suppose you're right," she said wearily, and we went into the living room, where we talked about other things, non-essentials, and at ten o'clock she threw me out. "Tomorrow's another working day," she reminded me. "And I got practically no sleep last night."

I kissed her good night, and she told me to be careful and then frowned, as though she were mad at herself for saying it. I promised her I'd be very careful, and then I went out to the car.

It was too early to go home. I drove over to the New Electric Diner, and Al and I had a grand time talking about the gouge in the formica. That killed an hour, and then I went home.

I got there about quarter past eleven. The grocery store was closed, but one light was still on, and inside I saw Joey Casale, cleaning the cold-cut slicer. I tapped on the window and waved, and he smiled and waved back. I went on upstairs.

I walked straight through the apartment to the kitchen, switching on lights as I went. I opened a can of beer, and then headed back toward the front of the apartment again. I opened the double doors leading to the den, switched on the light, and looked at a real mess.

I had had a visitor. He had been sloppy, and he had apparently been in a hurry. My desk drawers were scattered all over the floor, emptied onto the rug. The filing cabinet had gotten the same treatment, and the file drawers, now empty, were stacked haphazardly in a corner. The chair behind the desk was knocked over, the books had been swept off the bookshelves onto the floor, and the phone had, apparently for the hell of it, been ripped off the wall.

I'm grateful for that last item. If there hadn't been any mess in that room, I would have settled myself behind the desk, had some beer, and doodled awhile, trying to think. If the mess had been there but the phone was still working, I would have sat down behind the desk and called for some law.

As it was, I stayed just long enough to get a good look at the wreckage, and then I turned on my heel. I didn't even bother to switch the den light off. I went back to the stairs, shut the door behind me, and started down to call the cops from the store, thinking what a good thing it was Joey was still there.

I was halfway down when the explosion rocked the house. I lost my footing, slid down the rest of the way on my well-padded rump, somersaulted when I reached bottom, and came up hard against the front door.

14

PEEVISHLY, Harcum said, "You're causing me one hell of a lot of trouble, Tim."

"I'm real sorry," I said. I was still shaky, and it was the best I could do.

We were at the Winston General Hospital, where a man in white had put some goo on my head. I hadn't wanted to go to the hospital, since I could pretty nearly walk, but everybody had insisted. Now I was just glad to be alive and sitting down, and I didn't really care how much trouble I was causing Harcum. I'd lied when I told him I was sorry.

"Frankly," he said, "I was with Sherri."

"I'm with muscatel, myself," I told him. I wasn't thinking yet, I wasn't even trying to think. Breathing was plenty good enough for me right now. Thinking I could do later.

And old Joey Casale was dead. It was one of those stupid freak things. The grenade—that's what Hal Ganz had said it looked like, before Harcum had whisked me away to the hospital—had blown out the front windows, demolished the den furniture, and cracked the wall between den and staircase. It had also jounced all the furniture in the living room. It had jounced the sofa, and when the sofa landed, it knocked a huge chunk of plaster out of the grocery-store ceiling. Joey Casale had still been bent over the cold-cut slicer, cleaning it, and the plaster had caught him in the neck.

It was beginning to look as though I was a dangerous guy to be near.

It was now after two in the morning, and I'd been hours in that hospital. I had a neat new bandage on my head, and I was nervous and shaky, and they'd told me what my apartment looked like. And I wasn't ready to start thinking yet, or to try to answer Harcum with any degree of sense.

He sighed now, and got to his feet, and went over to the door. The man in white was in the next room, where I'd been patched up, and Harcum said to him, "Can Smith leave here now? Is he all right?"

The man in white—I didn't know if he was an orderly, a doctor, or what—came in and looked at me. He was in his late twenties, and looked tired and serious. "How do you feel?" he asked me.

"All right, I guess," I said. "A little shaky."

"You don't want to go to sleep yet," he said. "Not with that hit on the head. Stay up for a while, as long as you can. Drink coffee if you want, but no alcohol."

I nodded.

"Come back tomorrow afternoon to have that cut looked at and the bandage changed," he said.

"Okay."

"Come on," Harcum said. "My car's out front."

We left the white room and the white man and walked down the green-smelling corridor and out a door bracketed with red-lettered signs. The sign on the inside said EXIT. The sign on the outside said EMERGENCY ENTRANCE.

Harcum's car was a new Oldsmobile, two weeks old. Every June, when the prices on this year's model begin to drop, Harcum trades in last year's car for a new one, at Hutchinson's Auto Dealers, catty-corner across from City Hall. And any voter who thinks he does that on his salary also thinks the world is flat and is carried on the back of a turtle.

We climbed into the Olds, which still had that squeaky smell of newness, and Harcum purred it around the oval to the street. We traveled a dozen blocks or more before he made a wrong turn and wasn't heading toward my place anymore.

"Hey," I said. "I live back that way."

"I know where you live," he answered, but he didn't slow down or turn around or say anything else.

"What is this, Harcum? I live back that way."

"The doctor said you shouldn't go to sleep yet," he said.

"I can stay awake at my place," I told him.

He gave me a sour look, and went back to his driving. "You're a menace, Tim," he said. "You're a walking accident. I'm putting you in protective custody until morning."

"What the hell for?"

"So nobody else will get killed in your place," he said.

"You can't do this, Harcum," I told him, foolishly.

"Watch me," he said.

And I was still too woozy and shaken up to fight it. I lit a cigarette, leaned back in the corner, and wished the fog would clear up. It was too much effort to think or to argue.

Harcum drove downtown, stopped in front of City Hall, and walked me down the stairs to Police Headquarters in the basement. A three-handed game of pinochle was going on in one of the rooms beyond the main desk. Harcum sat me down at the table and said to the others, "Here's a fourth for you, boys. He got a knock on the head, so he isn't supposed to sleep for a while. And he isn't supposed to go home, either, not before morning."

"We can play double-deck," said one of the cops. It was Dan Archer, one of the two who had come to the diner last night, when this whole thing had started. And was that only last night? By God, it was.

Harcum went away, Dan produced another deck, and I sat watching him as he tried to shuffle ninety-six cards. He was my partner, and he dealt me a good hand, but I couldn't keep my mind on the game, so we didn't make our bid.

I played till five o'clock, lost seven bucks and change, and then I just couldn't keep my eyes open anymore. They promised to wake me at eight, and I went to sleep on a cot in the next room.

15

THEY LET ME SLEEP till noon. Then Andy Wycza, yet another of Jack Wycza's nepotic relations, woke me to tell me someone wanted to talk to me, in the office down the corridor.

I was ravenous, and had a throbbing headache, and I needed a shave, and the bastards were supposed to have awakened me at eight. I went grumbling down the hall to see who wanted what.

It was Dan Wanamaker and George Watkins, in person, in glorious Technicolor. George was mainly red and Dan was mainly green, but smiling.

"How's the miserable play, George?" I said.

"We wanted to talk to you, Tim," he said, too upset to think about plays.

"Before you did anything," added Dan. He smiled and smiled, and looked absolutely terrified. "Before you made any decisions," he explained.

"Then you're too late," I told them, and started out again.

"Wait!" Dan pleaded. "Tim, wait, please!"

I sighed and faced them again. "All right. What is it?"

"Will you wait for Jordan, Tim?" asked George. "Will you at least do that?"

"Why?"

"We know what you threatened—" Dan started, smiling, shaking.

I interrupted him, saying, "Not threatened. Promised."

He nodded violently, the smile expanding till it damn near filled the room. He was ready to agree with me all the way to hell. "We know you promised," he corrected himself, "to work with the CCG if there was another try, but—"

"And there was another try," I told him.

George said, "We can straighten it out, Tim. If you'll only wait for Jordan."

"*Wait* for Jordan?"

"Wait till he comes back," he explained.

I looked from one to the other. "Back from where?"

They exchanged glances, and George reluctantly said, "Albany."

I nodded. "So you tried Masetti, and he wouldn't go for it. So now Jordan's trying to talk business with the boss of the outfit, what's-his-name."

"Bruce Wheatley," piped Dan through his smile, eager to help.

"He'll be back by four, Tim," said George. "Will you wait till you talk to him?"

"Why?"

I swear to God, I thought Dan would split his head in two with that smile. "He'll be able to straighten it out, Tim," he said. "I know he will."

"It's only four hours," said George, hopefully.

"A lot could happen in four hours," I told him.

"Please, Tim," wheedled Dan. He was sweating, and growing greener by the minute, and he looked now like a beardless Santa Claus whose reindeer have just conked out at thirty thousand feet. And the smile was like a saber cut with teeth.

I chewed on my lower lip, thinking it out. I didn't particularly *want* to blow the whistle on this whole crowd. They were crooks, admittedly, but they kept a clean well-run up-to-date town, and I didn't see where their replacements, after a clean-up, would do much of a better job. If there was a way I could avoid blowing the whistle and still get the son of a bitch who had tried three times to kill me and succeeded instead in killing Joey Casale, I would very gratefully take that way.

So I finally nodded and said, "All right. Four o'clock. At his house."

Now George was smiling as much as Dan, and they were both talking at the same time. "Fine, Tim."

"Good boy, Tim." "You won't regret it, Tim." "I knew you'd listen to reason, Tim."

"Sure," I said. "But I still may go to Masetti at four-thirty."

16

THE FIRST THING I needed was food. I stopped in at the City Hall Diner, next door to Hutchinson's Auto Dealers, and had two cheeseburgers and three cups of coffee, and refused to talk about last night's explosion with Charlie, the counterman.

The next thing I needed was a shave and a change of clothes, and after that I needed wheels. So I grabbed a cab and headed home, and I refused to talk about last night's explosion with Barnie, the cab driver.

The apartment looked just as bad as the descriptions had led me to expect. I took one look at the former den, and carefully closed the doors on it. Somebody was going to pay for that, God damn it, and if the somebody had to be all of City Hall, that was just tough.

It was while I was shaving that I figured out where and how the guy would try next. He had to keep trying, he had to get me before four o'clock. I finished shaving, changed my clothes, got screwdriver, pliers and hammer from the tool drawer in the kitchen, half-filled a metal pail with water, and went downstairs.

I walked around the building to my Ford, put everything down on the ground, and very cautiously opened the hood. A shoebox, sealed shut with masking tape, was sitting on the block. A ragged hole had been punched in the top, and a couple of wires came out through the hole and went over to the terminals of the battery. Cute.

I went to work with the screwdriver, got the wires loose from the battery, and with all the care in the world lifted the shoebox out of the car. I turned, like a man balancing full coffee cups, and slowly lowered the shoebox into the bucket of water. Then I stood and looked at it, while bubbles streamed up through the wire-hole.

While I was standing there, I had a visitor. Bill Casale, old Joey's oldest grandson, a big and lumbering twenty-four-year-old, two months out of the Army. He was wearing Army khakis and a white T-shirt, he was smoking a cigarette, and he looked sore. It occurred to me all at once that the Casale family, for lack of a better target, might decide to blame me for what had happened to its patriarch. After all, he had been killed by a guy who was trying for me.

But I was wrong. Bill looked at me, at the open hood, at the tools on the ground, and at the shoebox in the water. After a minute, he said, "Another bomb?"

I nodded.

"He really wants you, doesn't he?"

"He really and truly does," I agreed.

"We want him, too," he said. "You know that."

"You and me both, Bill."

"When you find him," he said, "you let us know."

I shook my head. "When I find him, if I do, I let the law know. They'll take care of it."

"We'll do it better," he said.

"I'm sorry, Bill," I said.

He pulled a wrinkled envelope out of his hip pocket and held it out to me. "The family's hiring you," he said. "To find the old man's killer. When you find him, you let us know."

I looked at the envelope, and saw a hint of green behind the white paper. I could picture the family meeting—last night or early this morning—and the hat being passed, the collection taken up, Bill sent to give me the money, to be sure the Casale family got the man who had murdered old Joey, so he wouldn't be allowed to throw himself on the much tenderer mercies of the law.

"I'm sorry, Bill," I said again. "I can't do it."

He studied me for a minute, and then shrugged and dropped the envelope on the fender of the Ford. "You just let us know," he said, and walked away.

I stared after him. Everybody pushing me, everybody shoving me. I wasn't used to it, and I didn't like it a bit.

I didn't open the envelope. I just stuck it into the glove compartment of the Ford, slammed the hood, put the bucket of water and bomb on the floor in front, and drove very slowly downtown. I went to Police Headquarters first, left the bomb for the lab to look at, and drove on over to the office.

17

THE BURGLAR ALARM wasn't working. The first thing I noticed were the new scratches in the wood of the door, around the lock. I looked down at that for a few seconds, then raised my hand with the first key, planning to unlock the alarm box.

But I didn't have to. The metal front was scratched, bent out slightly by the lock. I pulled on it, and it opened.

The wiring inside was a mess. Wires were showing that were usually behind a metal plate, and there was a lot of electric tape wrapped around wires here and there, done slapdash, hurriedly.

Somebody had cut me out of the system, rewired so the alarm wasn't hooked up anymore. If they'd just cut the wiring, the alarm would have sounded at headquarters. But they'd kept the circuit closed by adding wiring and simply having the juice bypass my alarm.

I didn't waste time trying to unlock my door. I just pushed on it and it curved noiselessly back, and I went on in.

The filing cabinet had given the guy a lot of trouble. It was dented and battered, and the face had been knocked off the combination lock, and finally the guy had managed to slam the drawer-faces in far enough to insert a jimmy or a crowbar, and he'd literally torn the thing apart. The smashed drawers lay around on the floor, emptied, the remaining files strewn all over the place. It looked like Fifth Avenue after a confetti parade.

I sighed with relief, congratulating myself for having sense enough to move any of the files that might have proved useful to my caller. He'd undoubtedly tried here first. Not finding anything, he'd gone on to my place and torn *that* up. He still hadn't found anything, so he got mad and threw a grenade in the window after he saw me come home.

Now, if I only knew which of those files I'd moved was the one he'd been after . . .

The phone jangled, catching me off balance. I stared at it stupidly, and after a while it stopped, but I knew it was just inhaling, getting ready to jangle again.

In the interval, I took a second to wonder why he hadn't ripped the phone out here, as he'd done at my apartment. I supposed he hadn't been mad enough yet to wreck things for the sake of wrecking them.

Then the phone started again, and I stepped over a twisted drawer and picked it up.

It was Cathy, and she was screaming. "Where have you been? I've been calling and calling and calling."

"I just got to the office," I told her. I knew I should explain more than that, but I was looking at the wreckage that was supposed to have been an impregnable filing cabinet, and I was just a little too distracted.

"I heard there was an explosion," she said, rapid and excited. "I heard you'd been in an explosion, and you were taken to the hospital—"

"I just fell down and cut myself," I told her. "That's all. They let me out right away."

"I've been trying everywhere," she wailed. "Your home phone wasn't working, and nobody seemed to know where you were, and I've been going absolutely *frantic* here—"

So I told her about my night and my morning and what there'd been so far of my afternoon, and about Harcum keeping me in the clink overnight, and when I was finished, she said, "Tim, I'm scared."

"I've been scared for hours," I told her. I thought about the bomb in the car, which I hadn't told her about, and I knew it was true. I'd been scared for hours, and I'd been too keyed up to notice it.

"What are you going to do?" she asked me.

"At four o'clock I'm going to talk to Jordan Reed."

"What can he do? He promised you yesterday there wouldn't be anything else like this."

"I don't know what he can do," I told her truthfully.

"What if he can't do anything?"

"Then I go see Paul Masetti."

"You ought to go see him now," she said. "You ought to see him right away."

"I'll wait till after I talk to Jordan Reed," I said.

"Tim, you can't trust these people, you can't try to get along with them, it's too late to smooth things over."

I was afraid she was right, and I didn't want her to be right, so I got annoyed and said, "I'll handle it, Cathy. Don't worry about it, I can take care of myself."

"Tim, please. Listen to me."

"I'll pick you up at five o'clock," I told her. "I'll let you know what happened."

"Tim, please."

"I've got to hang up, Cathy," I said.

"Tim . . ."

I hung up, and stood looking out the window toward City Hall. Why had this all happened, why had the whole thing blown up in my face like this? I'd made the best deal I could, I'd balanced everything, worked to get along with everybody, worked to do my own job well and be both accepted and needed, and everything was going along fine. Everything had been going along fine for a decade and a half. And now it was all blowing up in my face.

The phone jangled again. My hand was still on the receiver, and I automatically picked it up, the second it started to ring. Then I regretted the movement, afraid it was Cathy again, with more of her fears and advice.

But it wasn't. A voice like gravel said, "Tim?"

"Yes," I said.

"Jack Wycza," he said. "What the hell is going on downtown?"

"Everything," I told him. "Or do you mean something in particular?"

"I mean Reed and that gang trying to crucify me," he said.

"I wouldn't be a bit surprised," I told him. "One of them is trying to murder me, so I don't suppose they'd stop at crucifying you."

"Listen," he said. He sounded harsh and frantic. "Listen, I don't like phones. Come out here. I got to talk to you, Tim, come on out here. Out to the candy store."

I had three hours before my meeting with Jordan Reed. It might not be a bad idea to be up on the North Side, away from my usual haunts, until the time to see Reed arrived.

"Tim, listen," he said into my hesitation. "I always played square with you, you know that. I've done you favors. You got to come out here."

"All right," I said.

"The candy store," he said again.

"I'll be right there," I told him.

I hung up, stepped over the demolished filing cabinet, and went out to the hall. I didn't bother to close the office door behind me.

I was midway down the hall when the elevator door slid open ahead of me and Harcum stepped out, with Ed Jason and Hal Ganz in his wake. I thought at first he had come up to see me, but the surprise and uneasiness on his face when he caught sight of me told me different.

"Hi, Tim," he said, awkwardly, and hurried on by me.

Hal Ganz gave me a big smile. "Well, Tim," he started, "we found the—"

"Shut up!" Harcum had wheeled around and was glaring at Hal.

Hal blinked and looked confused, but he didn't say any more.

"By the way, Harcum," I said. "You might take a look in my office while you're up here." Then I went on down to the elevator. Jack, the operator, was holding it for me. I stepped on board, and we dropped toward the street.

I wondered what Harcum had found, that he didn't want me to know about.

18

THE PEOPLE'S CANDY STORE was on Kosciusko Street, a street running up the side of one of the steepest hills in creation. Cars were parked up and down both sides of it, and I had to leave the Ford a block away and walk back down the hill to the store.

Inside, the People's Candy Store was just what it claimed to be, a candy store occupied by people. But it was other things, too. I stood by the candy counter while a couple of small fries made up their minds what to do with four cents, and then I told the proprietor, a short, shiny-spectacled, mustached little guy, "Jack Wycza's expecting me. Tim Smith."

"Mr. Smith," he said, the words heavily accented. "Yes, he told me. Go right on up." He pointed. "Through there, and up."

"Yes, I know."

I walked down the row of candy counters, through the door at the back, and into a room where eleven men with hats on their heads played poker at two large tables. A green shade over the lone window effectively kept out all daylight, and the room was lit by sixty-watt unshaded bulbs hung over each table. The air was blue with lazily hanging clouds of cigarette smoke. Coins tinkled and bills crackled, and the cards whispered as they were dealt.

Nobody paid me any attention, and I kept on going. A door in the right-hand wall opened on a flight of stairs. I climbed these to the horse-room on the second floor, which was now empty and dark, these windows, too, covered with dark green shades. I walked across the echoing wood floor to the door of Jack Wycza's office. The door was closed. I knocked on it, somebody said to come in, and I went in.

Jack Wycza was sitting behind an ancient wooden desk. Two other men leaned against the far wall, on either side of the room's lone window. A girl—I recognized her as yet another Wycza relative, a cousin of some kind named Cindy—sat in the room's only other chair, painting her nails with fire-engine-red polish.

Jack Wycza perfectly fitted the part of the ward politician, from the hat shoved far back on his shiny balding dome, through the stogie in his face and the white shirt open at the collar and the wide dark tie with the loose crooked knot, to the fat gut jutting out over his belt and the big soft hands unused to manual labor. His eyes were small and wide-set, squinting now from the cigar smoke, and his jowls were heavy and beard-stubbled. And for the first time since I'd known him, he looked scared.

He took the cigar out of his mouth and pointed it at me. "Tim," he said, and he had a slight trace of accent, though he'd been born in this country. "Tim, they asked you to finger me."

"News gets around fast," I said.

"You turned it down, huh?"

"Sure I did," I said.

He grinned happily and nodded. "You ain't working for them anymore," he said. "Ain't that right?"

"I've never been working for them," I told him. "I've never been working for anybody except me."

He stopped grinning. "What is this? What the hell are you talking about?"

I could have asked him the same thing, but I said, "I've never been one of that crowd. I've always been a free agent. I've worked with them, but that doesn't mean I'm one of them. Hell, I've worked with you, too. I've worked with just about everybody in this town."

"Tim, listen," he said, and he was being very solemn now, "listen, this ain't the time for that jazz. There's gonna be a war in this town, Tim, and everybody's got to line up, one way or the other. I heard about you turning them down when they wanted you to finger me to the reformers, so I figured you were quits with that crowd. I figured you'd be coming over with Abner Korlov and me." Abner Korlov owned Amalgamated Machine Parts, where most of the

North Side people worked. He and Jordan Reed had been bitter enemies for years. Reed had managed to grab control of the town, and Korlov had been trying ever since to get it away from him.

"You figured wrong, Jack," I said. "I'm not picking any sides."

"Tim," he said, "listen. I'm in a bind. Up here, I know where I am, I know what the score is. Downtown, I'm lost. It's out of my territory. Things have been okay up till now, but there's a war coming. And I don't have any contacts downtown."

"Your whole damn family works for the city," I reminded him.

He made a disgusted hand-motion. "They don't know from nothing. Everybody knows they're my people. Who talks to them, who tells them anything?" He frowned, then said, "Cindy, you two guys. Out a minute."

Without a word, Cindy and the two guys left the room, closing the door behind them.

Jack leaned forward, his belly against the desk, his face serious and worried. "I got to know what the downtown crowd is doing," he said urgently. "I was just lucky I heard about them asking you. That was just lucky. But I got to know what they're doing, what they're figuring. If I don't they'll crucify me. That's why I want you, I need somebody downtown. And I know if you said you were with me I could trust you."

"Jack—"

"Listen," he said. "A deal, we make a small deal. I do you a favor, you do me a favor. That's all there is to it. Okay?"

"What favor?" I asked him.

"You're downtown," he said. "You know what's going on. If you hear anything that's got to do with me, anything at all, you let me know. I'll keep it under my hat, I swear to God, nobody will ever know it came from you, not even my wife. A personal favor to me."

"Jack, listen—"

"Wait a second," he said quickly. "I'll give you something back. I'll do you a favor back. Somebody's been gunning for you, right?"

I nodded.

"You need a bodyguard," he said. "You need somebody to watch your back, watch your sides. Those two guys that were here, I'll have them stick with you. They're good, Tim, they know what they're doing."

The idea was awfully appealing. Though it might not be so good to have two of Jack's bully-boys on my flanks. "I don't know if I'll hear anything, Jack," I said. "Everybody's scared downtown, nobody's telling anybody anything."

"If you hear," he said. "You don't hear anything, okay, you don't. I'm not even asking you to go looking. Just if you happen to hear. And you got these two boys to help you."

I nodded. "All right," I said. "If I hear anything, I'll let you know. But don't count on me."

He grinned and leaned back in his chair. "They're good boys," he said. "They'll take good care of you."

"In what way, Jack?" I asked him.

He laughed. "Bodyguards walk in front, Tim," he said. "That's their job."

He hollered for everybody to come back in, and Cindy entered, followed by the two good boys. "Listen," Wycza said to them, "Tim's gonna help us a little bit, and we're gonna help him a little bit. Somebody's been gunning for him. I want you two to go with him, make sure he doesn't get hurt." He turned to me. "Tim, that's Ben and that's Art. They're good boys."

Ben was dead-pan, and simply nodded, but Art grinned like the Cheshire cat and said, "You sure you need bodyguards, Mr. Smith? You don't look like the type."

I touched the bandage on my forehead, and I thought of the four tries the guy had already made. "I'm pretty sure," I said.

19

W E WENT DOWN to the car, and the one named Art, the grinning one, slid into the front seat beside me, while the other one settled himself in back. I U-turned and headed back downtown.

After a couple of blocks, Art said, "Where we headed for, Mr. Smith?"

"Get some insurance," I said. "Make your job easier."

He grinned some more. "Jack told us you were shifty but honest," he said conversationally. "How do you work a stunt like that?"

"I'm on the side of the angels," I told him.

"There aren't any angels in Winston," he said. He reached out to flick on the car radio. "Mind some music?"

"That's a police radio," I told him. "All it picks up is squad-car calls."

He looked impressed. "How come you rate that?" he wanted to know.

"I'm on the city payroll," I told him. "I could have one of those things for my house if I wanted it."

"Wow," he said, in mock awe, and we rode the rest of the way in silence. I checked the rear-view mirror a couple of times, and Ben, the dead-pan one, just kept looking out the window at the houses as we went by. I wasn't sure whether he was being extra conscientious and was looking for possible snipers, or whether he was just bored.

Downtown, I found a parking space half a block from the Winston Hotel. "I've got to go talk to somebody in there," I told Art. "You and Ben can come along as far as the lobby, but from there on I walk alone."

"Sure thing, Mr. Smith," he said. "You're the boss." He unbent his lanky frame out of the car and strolled along beside me to the hotel. Ben kept a couple of paces behind all the way.

"Be right back," I said, when we were all in the lobby together, and went on to the desk. I got Masetti's room number from Charlie, the desk clerk, and took the elevator up to his floor. I followed the corridor around a couple of turns, and knocked on Masetti's door.

He opened the door right away, and looked at me as though he didn't at all like what he saw. I asked him if I could come in. He said, "Yes," and turned his back on me.

I went on into the room, and was surprised to see his suitcase, half-packed, lying open on the bed. Completely ignoring me, he went on with the process of transferring his clothes from the bureau to the suitcase.

I waited a minute for him to remember I was there, and when it became obvious that he wasn't going to remember, I reminded him, saying, "I'd like to talk to you, Mr. Masetti."

"Go ahead and talk," he said. He sounded peeved.

"I want to give you a piece of information," I told him, "if I can get a guarantee from you you won't use it until and unless I say you can."

"Is that right?" he said. He went on packing shirts, moving with the fast, unnecessarily rough movements of a man about to boil over with rage.

I didn't get it, and I didn't much like it. This wasn't the way I'd expected to find Masetti. I'd planned on telling him where the soup cartons full of files were hidden, if I could get a promise from him that he wouldn't make a move toward them unless I didn't call him at four o'clock. That way, I'd have double insurance against any double-cross from Jordan Reed. Because Jordan, after all, was one of the seven possibles on my suspect list.

But the way Masetti was acting, he couldn't care less if I talked to him or left or flew to the moon. It wasn't according to my plan, and it annoyed me.

"Look, God damn it," I said. "Are you going to listen to me, or aren't you?"

He turned then, and glared at me. "Mr. Smith," he said, "I don't frankly care what you do. You can tell me your little secrets if you want, or you can go to hell."

I blinked at him. "What the hell's the matter with you?"

"I've been replaced, that's what the hell's the matter with me," he said. "I am leaving this fetid little town you love so well. I am going back to Albany, on the three-fifteen train." He paused, glowered some more, seemed to think things over a bit, and added, "If you really have information, you can tell the other man when he gets here."

"Who is he," I asked, "and when does he arrive?"

"His name is Danile, Archer Danile. And he should be here by seven o'clock."

Seven o'clock wasn't much help to me. And if Masetti was leaving at three-fifteen, he wasn't going to be much help to me either. I'd just have to find somebody else to carry my insurance. Cathy, maybe. I'd thought of her before, and decided against it, partially because I didn't want to expose her to the possible risk in it, and partially because I didn't want to expose myself to another one of her lectures.

"All right," I said. "Thanks anyway."

"You are quite welcome," he said angrily, and went back to his packing.

And I went back to the lobby.

Art was still grinning when I got there. "Guess you won't be needing us anymore, Mr. Smith," he said.

I frowned at him. "Why not?"

"I called Jack while you were upstairs. He just heard on the radio, they arrested the guy who's been trying to kill you. Arrested him for the killing of the old guy in the grocery store."

I couldn't believe it. I hadn't thought Harcum would dare blow the whistle on one of his pals. "Who?" I demanded. "Who was it?"

"A lawyer," he said. "Ronald Lascow."

"Lascow!"

That stupid son of a bitch, that Harcum, he'd tried to palm the whole thing off on a fall guy! And he'd picked one of the few people in town I was absolutely sure couldn't possibly be the one who'd been after me. Ron Lascow. Harcum must be losing his mind, I thought, he must be losing his useless mind.

And then the other part of it hit me. It was on the radio, and they were specifically mentioning that he'd been arrested for the murder of Joey Casale.

The family, the Casale family. They were out buying the rope right now, I was as sure of that as I was sure that Ron Lascow was being framed.

That's what Hal Ganz had been going to tell me, up there outside the office! And no wonder Harcum had shut him up, because Harcum knew I wouldn't go for that for a minute.

I had to go over there and get Ron out, but that came second. The first thing I had to do was stop the Casales.

20

I KNEW where they'd be. Now that old Joey was dead, his oldest son, Mike, would be heading the clan. Mike and another son, Sal, ran a trucking company, and one of their warehouses would be the inevitable place for a family get-together.

I told Art that I'd still be needing him and Ben, that Harcum had tried to pin it all on the wrong guy, and the three of us left the hotel. We hurried down the street to the Ford, Art joined me in front again, and Ben, silent as ever, took up once more his half-asleep pose in back.

Casale Brothers, Moving and Storage, General Trucking, occupied a square block on Front Street, down a ways from the Reed & King Chemical Supplies Corporation plant. On this square block were four buildings, all old and tall and dirty and red brick, three of them with boarded-up windows. These three were the storage warehouses and the garage facilities. The fourth building, which still had glass in its ground-floor windows, held the offices. The rest of the block space was covered with asphalt and used for off-street parking of company cars and trucks, most of it enclosed by storm fencing.

I told Art and Ben to wait for me in the car. I didn't want Mike to get the idea I was coming to him with a show of force. "You're a busy busy man, Mr. Smith," Art told me, in that half-mocking half-impressed manner of his.

"Busy busy," I answered, and hurried away from the car toward the office building. I could feel Art's grin on my back.

The girl in the front office told me that Mike Casale, and the four other Casale brothers, and a few other people, were all over in the south building, but she wasn't sure I could get in to see them. I thanked her, told her I'd just stroll over and see for myself, and went back out to the sidewalk.

The south building was right next door, but the entrance to it was around in the back. I went through the passageway between the two buildings, turned the corner, and there was Bill Casale standing by the door, his arms folded across his chest, still wearing the khakis and T-shirt.

"Your father inside?" I asked him.

"He's busy right now, Tim," he said.

"I want to talk to him, Bill. He's making a mistake."

Bill didn't move a muscle. I was an outsider, not family, and only family could be trusted right now. "Let him decide that for himself," he told me.

"Bill, for Christ's sake, I'm on your side. You know that, for Christ's sake. Let me in to talk to your father."

"What about?"

"Ron Lascow didn't kill your grandfather," I told him.

"The radio said he did."

"And the newspapers said Dewey was President. Harcum's looking for a fall guy, that's all. This whole thing is mixed up with politics, and Harcum can't afford to dig too far."

"That isn't what the radio said," he insisted. "The radio said he tried to kill you because you found out about some sort of crooked tax deal he was trying to work up, and he was afraid you'd tell this reform group in town."

So now I knew why they'd picked Ron. They were going to try to make him stand double duty. The tax scheme was out the window, so they would make Ron do for the murder and also try to make him bear the brunt of the CCG investigation. And he was too recently one of the boys to be able to do much damage to them.

"It's a frame-up," I said. "Ron didn't kill anybody."

"The radio said he did," he said doggedly.

"For Christ's sake," I shouted, "what is the goddam radio, the voice of God? Harcum had to find a patsy, that's all. Bill, quit fooling around and let me talk to your father."

He shook his head. "Nobody goes in," he told me. "That's what they said, nobody goes in. And that includes you."

"Bill," I said desperately, "would I try to cover for Ron if he really was the guy who'd been trying to kill me? There were four goddam tries on my life, Bill. Use your goddam head."

"You could be wrong," he said.

"And I could be right," I told him.

He thought it over for a minute, and finally he said, "Wait here. I'll be right back."

"I'll wait," I promised him.

He went inside, and I heard the click of the door locking after him. I lit a cigarette and looked around at the parking lot. It was full, jammed with Casale Brothers trucks and with private cars. It looked as though the whole family must be inside, plus all the truckers working for the company. A small army. Enough to take Ron out of our rickety clink and hang him from one of the City Hall Park trees.

And Harcum wouldn't exactly overexert himself to keep Ron from being lynched. The murderer dead, saving the delicacy and embarrassment of a trial. Everything solved, and everybody happy.

Bill was gone only a minute or two. When he came back, he closed the door carefully behind him, looked at me, and shook his head. "He said no."

"Tell him to come out here, then," I said. "I've got to talk to him."

"He said no," Bill told me doggedly. "This is family business, and you stay out of it."

And the hell I would, too. I made a big show of reluctant departure, then scooted back down the alleyway to the street, Bill watching me every minute. I turned the corner, went back into the office building and said to the girl, "Mike sent me for a grommet."

"A what?"

"He told me where it is," I said, barreling around her desk. "Upstairs in the second flotsam on the right." I left her gaping at me, went through a door, down a hall, and up a flight of stairs.

I knew these buildings. I probably knew them better than Mike Casale did. He'd only been occupying the place for nine years, and before that it had been empty, and a bunch of car-parts-stealing kids had used it as a base. They'd had hub caps and mufflers and tail pipes hidden all over the place. Fred Hutchinson, of Hutchinson's Auto Dealers, had hired me to stop the thievery, and as a result of it I'd been all through these four buildings many times.

On the second floor, I turned right and found the wall I wanted, blocked by three high stacks of cartons. I was alone up here. It looked as though the whole crew was next door, tying the knot in the rope.

So I moved the cartons, which took a few minutes I didn't want to spare and most of my energy as well, and then I poked and pried at the plasterboard that covered the entrance.

Here on the second floor, there was an old enclosed walkway between the two buildings. It had grown too rickety to be safe, way back before the war, so both entrances had simply been covered with plasterboard and the walkway forgotten. This is where the kids had stored a lot of their loot.

By walking very slowly and carefully, precisely in the middle of the walkway, so my weight would be on the main beam, it was just barely possible for a chunky type like me to get across to the other building and lean against the plasterboard over there. Which led me to a dark, dusty, debris-filled, abandoned little storeroom with a solid and very securely locked door. All that physical labor for nothing.

No, not exactly. For I heard Mike Casale's voice, saying, ". . . then you guys with Sal go through those ground-floor windows around on the west side and . . ."

The voice was coming from my right. I headed that way, covered my hand with black crisscrosses by touching a ventilator grill, and said, "Damn!"

Mike's voice said, "What? What the hell was that?"

Not only could I hear him, he could hear me. And this, come to think of it, might be even better than face to face contact. No chance of his tying me up and leaving me here while he and his army went off to raise hell at City Hall.

"Mike!" I shouted.

"Who the hell is that?" he demanded. "Where are you?"

Another voice, fainter, said, "It's coming from the ventilator, Mike."

"There's somebody in the building!" shouted another voice.

"Mike," I hollered, "this is Tim Smith. I want to talk to you."

"Find that stupid bastard," said Mike.

"That's it, Mike," I said. "Waste your time. I want to talk to you, and I don't talk until everybody's in that one room.

"Where the hell *is* he?" cried a voice. "He can *see* us, for God's sake!"

Just go on thinking that, buddy, I thought happily, and said, "Let me know when you're ready to listen, Mike."

"Come out here and talk face to face, Tim," he snapped.

"Sure," I said, and laughed at him.

"If it's about Ron Lascow," he said, "you're wasting your time."

"And you're wasting your lives," I told him. "Ron didn't kill Joey."

"How come he's in jail for it?"

"He's the fall guy."

"Crap."

"You don't want to make a mistake, Mike," I said. "You want to be sure you know what you're doing."

"I know what I'm doing," he said.

"You ought to listen to me, Mike. I know more about this than you do."

Another voice—Mike's brother Sal, I thought—said, "We can't move till after dark anyways, Mike. Let's hear what he has to say."

"It won't make any difference," said a voice I didn't recognize. "He's just covering for Lascow. They're buddies."

"I wouldn't cover for a guy who'd tried four times to kill me," I said.

"All right," said Mike. "I'll listen. Come on out here and talk."

"I'll stay here, Mike, if you don't mind. I trust you, but I think you've got some firebrands there."

"Say what you've got to say, then," he said grumpily. And don't stall around forever."

So I leaned up against the wall, my mouth inches from the ventilator grill, and hollered for a while. I told them that Ron was being framed, and I told them why. I pointed out that the first attempt on my life had been made the night before Ron had even heard about the CCG, and that he and I had talked to the CCG representative together, and Ron had known he had nothing to fear from me.

When I was finished, there was silence for a minute, and I suddenly had the fear they'd all left while I'd been talking, that I was now all alone in this building, shouting out a long story with nobody around to hear me.

Then Mike said, slowly, "How do I know you're right? You *sound* right, you got a good line, but how do I *know*?"

So he was still there after all. "Because," I told him, "this is my business. Because I've been looking for the killer for the last two days, and if it had been Ron I'd have known about it long before this. And because you know how I felt about your father."

Another long silence, only this time I could hear the faint buzz of whispering. Then Mike came back. "All right," he said. "You've made your point."

"I'm glad to hear it," I said.

"One thing," he said. "We're still holding the rope. You point the finger, he's ours."

I really didn't care whose he was, so I wasn't about to argue the point. But there was a way I could now kill two birds with one stone. I wanted Mike to know for sure he could depend on me, and I wanted a side man I could trust more than Art and Ben. So I said, "I tell you what, Mike. You give me Bill, there. He can travel with me, see what I'm doing. And the minute I know for sure who it is, I'll give him the word. All right?"

The conference was briefer this time, and then Mike said, "You're on."

"My car's in front of your office," I said.

21

ART WAS ALONE in the car when I got back. I slid in behind the steering wheel and said, "Where's Ben?"

"I sent him for some cigarettes." He grinned and pulled a pack of cigarettes out of his pocket. Lighting one, he said, "I wanted to say one or two words to you in private."

"What kind of words?"

"Words that wouldn't get back to Jack Wycza."

"Such as?"

He seemed to think it over for a minute. At last he said, "I like you, Mr. Smith. I've heard some about you, before this, and I like what I heard. Shifty but honest. Everything's going to get jounced around in this town, but I have the feeling you're going to come out on top."

"I hope so," I said.

He glanced out the window. "I wouldn't trust Jack Wycza very far if I were you," he said.

"I don't intend to."

"It would probably help if you had somebody close to him, to let you know what's going on."

"It would at that. You applying for the job?"

He nodded, still looking out the window.

"Why?" I asked him.

"I like you, Mr. Smith," he said again. He looked back at me and grinned. "And I'd like to be with the guy who comes out on top."

"Here comes Ben," I warned him.

"Is it a deal? "he asked me.

"What do you want in trade?"

He shrugged. "I'm a very useful type, Mr. Smith. Whoever runs this town after this whole mess blows over will be able to use me. And you could be my character reference."

"That's all?"

"All."

Could I trust him? What the hell had made him offer the deal? But it didn't matter, I could agree and no harm done, whether I could trust him or not. And what good would it do me to say no?

Ben opened the back door on the street side, then, and slid in, reaching over to hand Art the pack of cigarettes. I said, "Then I think it's okay."

"Fine," he said. "Thanks for the cigarettes, Ben."

The other back door swung open, and I looked around to see Bill Casale climbing in. "Good to see you again, Bill," I said.

He was as dead-pan as ever. "Where were you hiding out, Tim?" he asked me.

"Remind me to tell you sometime. Bill Casale, this is Art and that's Ben."

They grunted at one another, and I started the Ford. Art said, "Where do we go from here, Mr. Smith?"

"Make another stab at getting that insurance," I told him. And, whether I liked it or not, the insurance was going to have to be underwritten by Cathy.

22

CATHY WAS BOILING, with that combination of fury and terror that only women really have down pat. I should have spent a while reassuring her, and apologizing to her for making her worry, and all that jazz, but I just didn't have the time or the patience for it.

"Yell at me later, Cathy," I told her. "I've got too many other things to do right now."

She stopped her yelling and studied me for a minute. "I want to know where you are," she said at last. "I want to know what's happening to you and what you're doing, and I want to hear about it from *you*. I don't want to come to work in the morning and have somebody else tell me you were involved in an explosion last night, and spend all morning going out of my mind, trying to find out where you are and how badly you're hurt and what's happened to you. I want you to *call* me."

"Cathy, I've been running around like a madman. I haven't had time—"

"Be quiet for a minute," she said. She wasn't yelling now, and she wasn't acting enraged. Instead, two high spots of color on her cheeks were the only physical signs that she was holding anger in. That, and her eyes and voice, both of which were cold and hard.

"I care about you, Tim," she said quietly, as though stating a rather unimportant fact. "I care about you, and so I want to know whether or not you're all right and safe. And I want to know that you care about me."

"Well, for God's sake, Cathy, I—"

"Just a minute," she said. "If you care for me, you'll want to spare me the kind of morning I spent today, if it's at all possible for you to do so. If you care for me, *you* will want to know that *I* am all right."

"Cathy, look—"

"If I don't mean anything to you," she went on, ignoring my interruption, "then just say so. Just say so right now, and we're finished. You don't worry about me and I don't worry about you and—"

"Cathy, wait," I said. I leaned down over the desk, taking her hands. "Listen, just because you're mad at me, don't throw the whole thing away. This last couple of days, I've been on the run in half a dozen different directions, not sure what's going to happen next, and I've been having trouble enough trying to think fast enough about all that's been going on, without trying to live a normal life on the side as well."

"A normal life? Tim, I simply ask that you *call* me—"

"Okay," I said. "I should have called you, and I didn't. I haven't been thinking about you as much as I should. For god's sake, Cathy, I haven't been thinking about *me* as much as I should. Wait till this goddam thing is over, will you? Don't expect me to act the way I normally would under circumstances like this."

She shook her head. "I don't see why you couldn't just pick up the telephone and call me," she said.

"Because I didn't *think* of it, God damn it! Because I'm trying to think of half a million things at once, and I didn't think about calling you. You want to make a whole soap opera out of it, for Christ's sake, go ahead. But at *least* wait until this thing is settled."

She nodded, but from the expression on her face I could tell she wasn't convinced. "All right," she said. "You didn't come here simply to see me. You don't have *time* for things like that. You came here because you want something from me. What is it?"

If I hadn't ignored the implication, we would have been off into another dandy little squabble, so instead I answered the question. "I have some files hidden, out at Joey Casale's grocery store. They're my ace in the hole. I want you to know where they are. If you don't hear from me by seven o'clock, you go to the Winston Hotel and ask for a guy named Danile. Archer Danile. You got the name?"

Her eyes were widening, but she didn't say anything, only nodded.

"You tell him where he can find the files," I said. *"If you don't hear from me before seven o'clock. If you do hear from me, you won't have to do anything. All right?"*

"Tim, what are you going to do?"

"Listen, now," I said. "The files are in two tomato soup cartons, in the storeroom at the back of the grocery store, to the right as you face the front of the store. Have you got that?"

"What. Are. You. Going. To. Do?"

"I have an appointment with Jordan Reed," I told her. "I want the word to get around that I have insurance, that killing me won't stop those files from going to the CCG."

"Tim—" She was going to start the other routine now, she was going to be afraid for me, out loud.

I didn't have time for that, either. "I'll see you sometime before seven," I said, and headed for the door.

She talked at my back until I was out of the office. I was afraid she'd follow me out to the hall, but she didn't. I took the creaky old elevator back downstairs, left City Hall, and returned to the car and my three cronies. It was nearing four o'clock. I made a U-turn and drove toward Jordan Reed's place.

23

I F YOU LOOK at a map of the town of Winston, it will probably strike you right away that the town is shaped like a balloon on a string, and if you happen to know the particulars of the case, the symbolism of that won't escape you.

The balloon itself is the main area of the town, the business and residential and industrial districts. The string is a two-lane blacktop road headed northwest into the Adirondacks, called McGraw's Market Road. I doubt that anybody anymore knows who McGraw was or what kind of market he had. And at the end of the string, where the owner of the balloon would be holding it, that's where Jordan Reed's estate is.

Reed bought the estate around twenty years ago, and at that time the place was a good five miles from the city line. Which meant it wasn't hooked up to the town sewage system or water mains, and the county rather than the city had the responsibility for keeping McGraw's Market Road free of potholes and frost heaves. Two years after Reed moved in, the City Council unanimously agreed that that five-mile stretch of McGraw's Market Road was really a part of Winston after all.

The house itself was set back a quarter-mile from the road on a slim plateau midway up Claridge Mountain. The whole plateau, maybe a couple miles long and half a mile wide, was the Reed estate, heavily forested and securely fenced. One turned right from McGraw's Market Road, past two massive stone gateposts, and dead ahead a quarter of a mile on blacktop through the trees to the house.

The house was one of those big rambling monstrosities built at a time when bay windows and corner towers and rococo wood curlicues were all the rage. The first-floor exterior was of stone, the two floors above it faced with gray shingles. The roof slanted this way and that over the various wings and outcroppings of the place, and a wide screened porch surrounded the first floor on three sides.

I pulled the Ford onto the dirt beside the house, where guests were supposed to park, told my crowd to wait for me, and walked over to the house.

The porch was cool and dim. Woven straw rugs crackled underfoot, and whitewashed tables and chairs were off to the left, with an old crank-'em-up phonograph which now, its guts removed, served as a liquor cabinet.

I rang the bell and waited, listening to the silence. The trees were rustling a little bit, but that was all the noise there was in the world.

A maid opened the door, finally, and said, "Mr. Smith, yes. Mr. Reed said you'd be calling. This way, please."

I followed her inside and through the long, cool rooms. Jordan Reed himself was the modern businessman, dressed to the minute, completely up to date in both his business and social life. His plant was so modern it was painful. But his home was a cool, dim breeze straight out of the nineteenth century.

We walked back through the house, through rooms muffled by deep-piled Oriental carpets, the wall mirrors gleaming dark, the rich woods of the furniture burnished to warm highlights, the ceilings high and dim, the walls papered with gentlemen and ladies riding in carriages or sitting quite formally in tiny rose arbors. There were no halls or corridors in this house, at least not on the first floor. One simply walked from room to room, through doorways graced with heavy, polished, intricately carved doors.

I half-expected to see Marvin Reed lurking in a corner of one of these rooms, still hiding from the by-now-departed Paul Masetti, but aside from the stolidly waddling maid, I saw no one, not Marvin or his wife Alisan or any other servants.

We stopped, finally, before one of the most rococo doors this side of the nearest cathedral, and the maid tapped diffidently on a curlicue. A muffled sound from inside might have been instructions to enter. The maid opened the door, ushered me in, closed the door again, and presumably went away.

This was Jordan Reed's den, and a fantastic room it was. For some reason, that den always seemed to emphasize my chunkiness. The wall directly opposite me as I walked in was almost completely glass, two high wide windows looking out across the cleared side lawn and down the long forested slope of Claridge Mountain to the valley, where the whole town was laid out like a model on a table top. Between the windows was a six-foot-wide strip of wall, dominated by a frowning dark gloomy oil painting of Jordan Reed's father Jonas, who, with Michael King, founded Reed & King Chemicals back before the turn of the century. The entire left wall, side to side and floor to ceiling, was lined with bookshelves, with the old morocco-bound matched sets on the upper shelves leading down through grim-colored texts on business and finance and American tax structure, through gaily dust-jacketed novels bought by Jordan's late wife via mail-order book clubs, down to the bottom shelf way over on the right where red and yellow paperback books were not quite hidden from view. The right-hand wall held photographic blowups of the Reed & King plant and various members of both families, over a leather davenport, a couple of ashtray stands and a well-stocked liquor cabinet. Brown leather armchairs flanked the doorway, with a map of Winston on the wall to the left of the door and a genealogical chart of the Reed clan to the right.

In the center of all this was a huge U-shaped desk, custom-made to Jordan Reed's own plans, with Reed himself at the chair in the middle of the U, sitting with a loose-leaf notebook open in front of him, making notations in it from a sheet of paper to his right.

He looked up at my entrance, his face bland and smiling. "Ah, Tim," he said, getting to his feet and backing out of the U. "Scotch," he asked me, "or rye?"

"Neither," I said. "Talk."

He frowned, paused midway to the liquor cabinet, studying me. "All right," he said. "Sit down, Tim."

"I'll stand."

"Oh, come on, Tim, don't have a chip on your shoulder." I'd expected him to be just a little bit worried. This bland good humor had *me* worried. "Do you remember," I asked him, "what I promised yesterday?"

He nodded. "Of course," he said, and continued on to the liquor cabinet. "You threatened to go to the CCG," he said, "if there were any more attempts on your life."

"And there was another one last night," I said. "Wanamaker and Watkins asked me to wait until I talked to you."

He nodded, and mixed himself a drink, moving slowly, and not looking at me again until the drink was ready. Then he glanced over and said, "You waited. And it's a good thing you did, since now it's pretty plain you had the wrong idea."

"Which wrong idea was that?"

"That it was one of the people at that meeting," he said. Behind the bland smile, he was watching me.

I held it in, trying to be as matter-of-fact as possible. "That isn't pretty plain to me," I said.

He did a creditable job of looking surprised. "But Harcum has made an arrest," he said.

I laughed in his face, and the laughter was mainly from relief. He had been acting so cool, so pleased with himself, I'd been worried he had some ace up his sleeve, some way to cancel me out as a threat. But all he had was Ron Lascow!

He looked hurt. "I don't see anything funny, Tim," he said.

"Neither do I," I told him. "Not really. Harcum's working out of desperation. He thinks he can frame Ron, and he's crazy."

"Not necessarily, Tim. I've talked with Harcum, briefly, and it does all hang together. Lascow had opportunity—"

"So did a lot of other people."

"Of course. And he also had just as much motive as anybody at City Hall. And he *wasn't* one of the people to whom you delivered your ultimatum. Believe me, Tim, we all know you don't make empty threats. None of us would—"

"Stop it, Jordan," I said. "It's one of you seven, and you know it. Do you have anything sensible to talk about, or should I just go away and chat with the CCG?"

He shrugged, not looking worried at all. "I had assumed," he said, strolling across the den, "that Lascow's arrest was the end of all this trouble, and we'd be able to concern ourselves with the CCG from now on." He paused in front of the genealogical chart, and reached up to tap it. "I've left a lot of room there," he said. He turned to look at me, smiling. "Think I'll make a good grandpa?"

He was too damn sure of himself. I said, "You went to Albany to see Bruce Wheatley, the head of the CCG. Did you manage a deal?"

"Of course not," he said. He looked back at the chart again. There were Reeds listed as far back as 1734. William begat Francis, and Francis begat Hiram, and Hiram begat Lawrence, and on and on it went, until finally Jonas begat Jordan and Jordan begat Marvin, and Marvin didn't beget anybody. I knew that bothered Jordan. Jonas had left the firm to Jordan, who would leave it to Marvin, and he wanted to know that Marvin would be leaving it to another Reed. I had the feeling Jordan had managed to ignore an awful lot of Marvin's weaknesses, just for this reason. I also had the feeling that Jordan was unaware that Marvin had done most of his sowing in recent years away from home. If Jordan had learned that, Marvin would have been out on his ear, and not because Jordan is a prude, which he isn't, but because Marvin could sow his wild oats only *after* he had fulfilled the begat requirement.

Jordan turned away from the chart and amplified his last statement. "The CCG," he said, "is unfortunately honest."

"I'm glad to hear that, Jordan," I said. "Because I'm on my way to join them."

He raised an eyebrow, but seemed otherwise unruffled by my news. "Tim," he said, "are you sure you've thought this out?"

"What do you think?"

I think there may be one or two points you haven't Considered," he said.

"Such as?

"If you turn on your friends," he said, "they'll turn on you. Remember, you're just as implicated as anyone else. You've withheld evidence of crimes."

I shook my head. "You're wrong. I can't be called on that after I've stopped withholding. The minute I turn my files over to the CCG, I'm clear."

"If you do this, Tim," he said, "you're through in Winston, I hope you realize that. No one will be able to trust you anymore. And you have to be trusted to stay in business."

"Given the choice between living and being trusted," I told him, "I'll pick living every time."

He shrugged. "All right," he said. "You're going to be obstinate. I don't know why you waited to talk to me. There's nothing I can say more than what I've already said."

"You can say," I told him, "that you guarantee to have the killer behind bars within the hour. You can say that Ron Lascow will be released one phone call from now."

He shook his head. "I can't do either, Tim," he said. "They're contradictory. Whether you like it or not, Ron Lascow is the man."

At this point, it was obvious that the only thing for me to do was go away. He was harping on Ron, and letting me know that he wasn't worried by anything I might do. Either he was lying, and he'd managed to wangle a deal directly with the CCG after all, or his trip to Albany had resulted in his reaching somebody high enough in the state government to offer him protection from the reformers.

"All right, Jordan," I said. "They asked me to talk with you. I've talked with you."

"Yes, you have," he said blandly.

"I think you ought to know," I said, "that my files are in safe place. If anything happens to me, a friend of mine will turn them over to the CCG anyway."

He shrugged. "As far as I'm concerned," he said, "you're perfectly safe."

While he was talking, there was a faint rap on the door. He frowned, called an order to come in, and the maid appeared in the doorway, white-faced and wide-eyed. "Mr. Jordan," she whispered. She glanced at me, and bugged her eyes at her employer some more. It was plain they both wanted me to leave. So I left.

24

I RACED through the house toward the front door, wondering what that maid had been so upset about and hoping it didn't have anything to do with me. And I was all the way into the room where Alisan Reed was sitting crying before I even noticed she was there. I said, "Whoops!" and back-pedaled.

She looked up at me, her patrician face marred by tear stains and frown lines and a shiny nose, and she said, "Tim Smith! What are you doing here?"

"Getting nowhere with your father-in-law," I said.

"Him." The first pronoun insult I'd ever heard.

"What's the matter, Alisan?" I asked her. We'd never known each other very well—she wasn't a Winston girl to begin with, but something Marvin had brought back from college with his diploma—but it would have been ridiculous to call her Mrs. Reed at that moment.

"After the kind of son *he* produced in Marvin," she said bitterly, "you'd think he'd be grateful there weren't any more children in the line."

I looked at her closely, and now I saw that she'd been crying tears of frustrated fury and not of sorrow. "He's nagging at you for a grandson, huh?"

"Me!" she cried in rage. "Not Marvin, ever, only me!" She got to her feet, trembling with fury now, and I could see she was delighted at the chance to do some hollering. "Let me tell you something," she said tightly. "Something *he* doesn't seem to realize. Before you can have any children, you have to have sexual intercourse."

"Uh," I said. It was the most comprehensive answer to that little comment I could think of. I started edging toward the opposite door. "Well, uh—" I said, in amplification.

She shook her head, rubbing her forehead with the heel of one hand. "Oh, I'm sorry," she said angrily. "Never mind me. It was just that he came back from Albany— You'd think he was a feudal baron, the way he carried on."

So it *was* in Albany that the change had taken place, whatever had changed that had made me no longer a threat. "I've got to get going, Alisan," I said hastily. "I'm sorry, uh—"

"Oh, go on," she said. "I didn't mean to make a fool of myself. Go on."

I went on. Outside, it was still a summer afternoon, moving slowly now toward evening. I stood on the screened-in porch for a minute, looking out at nothing in particular, thinking about how much I would have given to have heard that maid's news, and wondering just what had happened in Albany that had shuffled me out of the deck, when Reed's gardener-handyman, a grizzled, toothless, disgruntled old geezer, went trotting by at what was for him top speed, pausing only to glower at me suspiciously before disappearing around the corner of the house.

I left the porch and went back to the car. As I slid in behind the wheel, Art said, "What's the good word, Mr. Smith?"

"I don't think there is any," I said. I jabbed the key into the ignition, started the engine, and said, "Let's all go visit Ron Lascow. You got the saw with the cake baked in it?"

They laughed without understanding what they were laughing about, only understanding that I had said something funny and that I was in a dangerous mood, so it was a good idea for them to laugh, and then we drove away from Reed's house, along Reed's private road through Reed's private woods and so back to McGraw's Market Road.

Where we were stopped by three siren-blaring police cars just making the turn, and a plainclothes detective named Ed Jason stuck his head out the window to shout, "Okay, Tim, turn around and go back. Nobody leaves this property yet."

Art, beside me on the front seat, said, "Now, what the hell is that all about?"

He didn't get any answers.

25

It was a hell of a long quarter-mile back to the house. I had plenty of time to think, and plenty of uncomfortable notions to think about.

Jordan Reed hadn't been worried. I had promised him that I was on my way to the CCG with enough information to turn City Hall upside down and shake it like shaking dirty socks out of a laundry bag, and he hadn't been worried. I'd seen two possibilities for that—he'd made a deal with the CCG or he'd managed to make a deal higher up and pull the reformers' sting—but not until right now did I see the third possibility.

That I'd never get back to town.

But there was the maid breaking into Reed's office, and the funny look the gardener had given me. This might be something else entirely.

I had three men with me in the car. Bill was unarmed, and he was a noncombatant anyway. Art and Ben were armed, but whose side were they on? I'd let them flank me all afternoon, and what the hell did I know about them, or what the hell did I know about what Jack Wycza was planning?

I was an idiot.

I'd just about come to that decision when we reached the house again, and I braked to a stop. Two of the police cars passed me, parking just ahead, and the third stopped against my rear bumper.

I sat tense, both hands still holding the wheel, high up, where I wouldn't have far to move to get inside my coat. I looked straight out the windshield and said, "Stay in the car. Let them make all the first moves."

Nobody answered me.

Up ahead, car doors were opening and spilling out Winston's finest. I heard the chatter of a police radio, and wanted to switch on my own radio and listen in on the calls, but it seemed somehow like a bad time to do it.

Ed Jason came strolling back toward me, paused by the fender, looked in through the windshield at me, and suddenly grinned. "Take it easy, Tim," he said. "We're not saying you did it. You're just all maybe witnesses, that's all."

"Did what? "I asked him.

"Killed her," he said.

"Killed who?"

He shrugged. "Don't know yet. You fellas just sit tight in the car. Harcum'll be along pretty soon." And he moseyed—there's just no other word for Ed Jason's walk—off toward the house.

Beside me, Art said, "Here."

I looked at him, and he was offering me a fresh-lit cigarette. I grinned, spastically, letting all the tension out, and took the cigarette from him. I said, "Thanks."

Bill Casale, in the back seat, said, "What's going on?"

"You've got me, Billy boy," I told him. I felt very good, very expansive. "It doesn't concern us," I said, "that's all that matters to me."

Art said, "Shall we get our stories straight?"

"What stories?" I asked him. "We don't know anything. Did you guys see any woman getting killed?"

Art said, "No." Bill said, "I didn't see anybody except that old man, when you were on the porch." Ben didn't say anything. Ben *never* said anything.

"Well, then," I said.

"What were we all doing here?" Art asked me.

"The truth," I said. He raised an eyebrow, but he let it go at that.

We sat around, watching, and after a while I figured it out that the main area of interest was around on the other side of the house. The chain of events seemed clear, up to a point. The gardener had been over on that side of the house, had seen the dead woman, had rushed into the house and informed the maid, and she had come charging in to tell Reed just as I was leaving. Reed had quick called the law, while I was chatting with Alisan and standing around on the front porch, and by the time I'd driven out to the highway, the law had arrived.

It was clear, as I say, up to a point. Then it got muddy. For instance, who was this dead woman? Not Alisan, obviously, since I'd just talked with her. And not the maid either. And I didn't know of any other women who lived in this house.

And, just incidentally, who had killed her? And why had it happened on the Reed estate?

I stewed on those questions for maybe half an hour, and finally Harcum arrived. He conferred with Ed Jason for a while, up on the front porch, and then Ed moseyed on over and said to me, "Harcum wants a chat."

"All of us?"

"He just mentioned you."

So the others waited, and I went up on the porch to talk to Harcum. Ed Jason headed back around the corner of the house like a cowboy going to the corral.

The porch was what you might call crowded. Harcum was there, and so was Jordan Reed, and so was Marvin Reed, and so was Alisan Reed. Marvin looked baffled, Harcum angry, Jordan angrier, and Alisan angriest.

Harcum said, when I was halfway through the screen door onto the porch, "Any of your bunch see her at all?"

I shook my head. "I didn't. I asked the others, and they didn't either."

"From the spot where she was killed," said Jordan Reed tightly, "she walked in from the highway, took the dirt-path short cut through the trees. You wouldn't have seen her from the front of the house at all."

"We're trying to find out if anybody saw who she left the hotel with," said Harcum.

"Isn't that obvious?" asked Jordan Reed bitterly. "She left alone, probably took a cab, and walked in from the highway because she didn't want anyone else to see her." He flashed a bitter glance at his son. "I suppose she'd been here before," he said. "When I was away on business."

"Never!" cried Marvin. He still looked baffled, but now he looked a bit scared as well.

"I suppose," said Jordan, "neither of you expected me back from Albany so early."

"I didn't even know she was in town!" cried Marvin hopelessly. "I haven't seen her for years!"

"You wanted to know why I didn't give you a grandson," said Alisan, her voice harsh and vicious. "Now you know why. I don't have to hide it anymore."

"Alisan!" cried Marvin, like a drowning man calling for a life preserver he doesn't really expect to get.

"I knew Sherri used to know Marv—" started Harcum, and I inadvertently interrupted him, blurting, "Sherri!"

He glanced over at me, somber and frowning. "Yes, Sherri," he said.

Oh ho, I thought. Oh ho de ho ho. The dead woman was Sherri, who used to know Marvin Reed, and who had come to town with Harcum— I could see why Harcum was so gloomy. It isn't pleasant to realize you were just a railroad ticket. Sherri had come to town to see Marvin again, and if I'd figured Sherri right she spelled Marvin with a capital $.

Had she seen him?

The cluck in question was saying, "Dad, I haven't seen her for years, I swear it, not for years."

Jordan looked at his son the way he'd look at a New Dealer, and said, "You're scum." And then he looked away again. Never had a son been disinherited so briefly or so completely.

Harcum caught that message, too, and took courage from it. To Marvin, he said, "It looks like you're the prime suspect, boy. And the only suspect."

"But I didn't *see* her!" Marvin wailed. "I swear it, I swear it, I never even *saw* her!"

"What was the weapon?" I asked.

Harcum pointed at the whitewashed porch table. There was something on it, wrapped in a white handkerchief. I went over to inspect. Harcum was so used to me nosing around he didn't make a murmur.

It was a bone-handled hunting knife, balanced, with a thick blade six inches long. Sheldon's, the big department store downtown, sold that particular model by the carload lot. Winston is a big hunting town, and this was one of the most popular hunting knives.

"What about prints?" I asked.

Harcum snorted. "On that handle?"

He was right, come to think of it. A rough, grainy surface like the handle of that knife wouldn't produce a print in a million years.

Harcum was saying, "You want to tell us about it, Marv? She came up here to talk to you. She wanted money, I guess. You couldn't afford what she wanted, and you were afraid your father would see her. So you killed her, and you were going to get rid of the body but the gardener came along first, scaring you off. Is that the way it happened?"

Marvin just stared at Harcum, shaking his head slightly, and then he turned to his father, who was glaring out over the wooded slope at the town. "Dad," he said. "Dad, please."

Jordan didn't move.

"Dad, please," said Marvin, "I didn't do it. I haven't seen her for years, I— Dad, *listen* to me! I'd do anything for you, you know that. I haven't seen her for years."

He stopped, his hands working jerkily in his lap. He looked pleadingly at me, at Harcum, even at Alisan. "Anything," he said. "I didn't do it."

It was uncomfortable as hell, for everybody concerned, and we were all grateful for the interruption when the silence following Marvin's plea was broken by the screen door opening.

It was Art, looking in with polite apology, saying, "You okay, Mr. Smith?"

"I'm peachy," I told him.

He took that at face value, and said, to the group in general, "Is it all right if I use the phone?"

Jordan turned away from glaring at the town to glare at Art, a who-the-hell-are-you glare, and then he shrugged. "Go ahead."

"Thanks." Art came in the rest of the way and said to me, in a somewhat lower voice, "Got to check in with Jack again."

He went on into the house, and Harcum cleared his throat portentously. "It seems like a pretty clear case to me, Marv," he said. "You sure you don't want to talk about it?"

Before Marvin could answer, I got to my feet and said to Harcum, "Can I talk to you for a second?"

He frowned at me. "What the hell is it, Tim?"

"Just take a second," I said.

Grumbling, he followed me along the porch and around the corner, out of sight and hearing of the family group back there. I said, "Let me do you a favor, Harcum. Jordan just might reconsider. You better take it easy with Marvin."

"It's an open-and-shut case, Tim," he said.

I shook my head. "It's an *obvious* case," I told him. "But it isn't open-and-shut. You don't have any witnesses, you'll never trace that knife back to Marvin in a million years, and you don't know for sure that she even *got* to Marvin."

"I got a good circumstantial case—" he started.

"You don't have any case at all," I told him. "A good defense lawyer will run your case right out of court. And if Jordan reconsiders, Marvin will *have* a good defense lawyer."

"Then what the hell am I supposed to do?" he demanded.

"Take it easy," I advised him, "and let your detectives handle this. That's what the city pays them for. You've already made one stupid arrest—"

"You mean Lascow? I've got a case against him, by God."

"And the hell you do, too."

"I've got a case!" he insisted.

"I'd sure like to see it," I said.

"You'll see it," he said darkly. "You might like to know what Lascow's job is in the National Guard."

I blinked. I knew Ron was a lieutenant in the Guard— it kept him from active duty—but I didn't see what the hell that had to do with the price of beans. "I give up," I said. "What is his job with the National Guard?"

"He's in charge of a bomb demolition squad," he said, 'They taught him all about taking bombs apart. And putting them back together again."

I stared at him. "Is that all you've got?"

"Not by a long shot." He pushed past me, the conversation finished for now, and went back to the Reeds, where he started telling Marvin how he shouldn't leave town or anything, that although he wasn't under arrest he would probably be wanted for questioning and he should keep himself available and—

I broke in, saying, "You want me to stick around here anymore?"

He looked at me, thrown off the track. "Hell, no," he said, and went back to Marvin, trying to remember where he'd left off.

"Keep yourself available," I prompted, collected my dirty look, and went back to the car.

Art hadn't returned yet, so I sat there and answered Bill's questions for a while. Then Art came strolling toward the car, frowning, his usual sardonic smile missing from his face. He slid into the front seat beside me and said, "There've been some changes, Mr. Smith."

"Such as?"

"Jack says for me and Ben to come on back in."

"Why?"

He shrugged. "It looks like the arrangement between you and *him* is all finished." Meaning that our own private arrangement was still alive.

"He wants you right away?"

"Right away," he said.

I wondered if this move had anything to do with Reed's earlier smugness. I had the feeling in the small of my back that it did.

"Just in case he changes his mind again," said Art casually, "where do we get in touch with you?"

I wasn't sure myself. I still didn't have a working phone at home, and I'd be pretty much on the move from now on. I finally decided on Cathy's place, figuring she could take a message if I wasn't there.

He took down the address and number and said, "Mind dropping us off in town?"

"Not at all."

This time, we got to the highway with no interference, and I went a couple blocks out of the way to drop Art and Ben off in front of the People's Candy Store. Bill switched to the front seat, and we drove on down toward the center of town.

26

"I'M WORRIED, Tim," said Ron Lascow. "At first, I thought Harcum was crazy, he'd never make the charge stick. But now I'm not so sure."

We were sitting in the Visitors' Room in the Winston City Jail, a buggy-whip era clink that took up half of the basement of City Hall. There was none of the wire mesh separating me from Ron that they have in the big city jails and the state and federal penitentiaries. The Visitors' Room was simply a bare square room with cream-colored walls and four of the old wooden chairs that used to be upstairs in City Court. The door to the cell area was open. The other door was closed and locked, but it was simply a wooden door with an ordinary Yale lock on it.

All four chairs were occupied at the moment. There was Ron, and Bill Casale, and a cop named Titus O'Herne, and me.

"Why aren't you sure?" I asked him. "There isn't a bit of evidence against you."

"There's that tax-scheme thing," he said.

"So what? I already knew about that. You knew you were safe from me, you had no reason to want to kill me."

He nodded, and rubbed a hand wearily over his face. He was wearing brown slacks and a white shirt open at the collar, the sleeves rolled up. Just the fact of being in jail, innocent or not, had taken a lot of starch out of him. "I don't have any alibi for the time when the grenade was thrown," he said. "I was home, alone."

"So were a lot of people," I told him. "So was I, for that matter. And I know about the National Guard thing, the bomb demolition squad. That maybe gives you the method for the bomb in the car, but not for the hand grenade."

His grin was sick. "Sure it does," he said.

"How so?"

"The Guard isn't as tight as the regular Army," he said. "I mean the controls aren't as good. And you've got a bunch of young kids in there. Every summer, during the two weeks at camp, something disappears from the armory. A gun, or a grenade, or maybe just a holster. But always something."

"So if the whole damn Guard is short one hand grenade," I said, "they'll try to pin it on you?"

"They've got it all, Tim," he said. "Not enough to convince you, maybe, because you know me, and you're on my side. But whose side is the judge going to be on? And they've got it all, motive and method and opportunity."

"What about the other tries?" I demanded. "What about the Tarker killing? Or the shots fired at me from City Hall?"

He shook his head. "I won't be charged with trying to kill you," he said. He nodded at Bill. "I'll be charged with killing his grandfather."

"While *trying* to kill me," I insisted.

"Sure," he said. "And if the defense even does succeed in getting the other tries admitted, what good does that do me? I've been to New York in the last three months, so I could have hired that gunman. And I was home alone when *he* was killed, too. And when you were being shot at from City Hall, I was driving out to Hillview. Alone."

"He has less of a case against you than he does against Marvin Reed," I said.

He looked blank. "Marvin Reed?"

I told him about the killing of Sherri, and he said, "Jesus, it's catching. Who would have thought little Marvy had the guts?"

"Maybe he didn't do it," I said.

"Sure. And maybe pigs fly." He got to his feet, paced nervously back and forth in the small room, his arms swinging with nervous tension at his sides, *"He* ought to be in here," he said. "Not me, for Christ's sake."

"Who's your lawyer?" I asked him.

"Stanley Crawford."

I nodded. Crawford was an old man, in semi-retirement now, who had first encouraged Ron to study law. He was able, but slow-moving, having long since adapted himself to the snail's pace of the law.

"What's he doing about getting you out of here?" I asked.

"He's trying to get Judge Lowry to set bail. I don't know, he said he'd come down and see me this evening."

"I don't like to rush you fellers," said Titus O'Herne, the guard, "but I would like to get this felon here back behind bars, so I could go get me some chow." Titus was a short, grizzled, toothless old duffer, given duty here in the town clink when he got too old to walk a beat anymore.

I looked at him. "You alone here?"

"Damn right," he said.

"For how long?"

He grimaced. "Forever, from the looks of things," he said. "I should of been off duty at five o'clock, dang near an hour ago."

"Then why aren't you?"

"Young Ed Wycza was supposed to take over from me," he explained. "But he walked off with the rest of the family."

I came to attention, hearing the clang of a warning bell. "They walked off?"

He nodded sourly. "The whole dang family," he said. "Just a little before four. They all just up and walked off, without a by-your-leave to anybody."

"What's happening out there, Tim?" Ron asked me.

I looked at him and shook my head. "I don't know. A war, I think. And I'm no longer sure who's on what team."

"If Jack Wycza marches his people after Jordan Reed and the others . . ." He left the sentence unfinished.

I finished it for him. "If he does," I said, "he'll solve every one of our problems for us."

"Maybe Jordan's out of it anyway," he said, "now that his son is in trouble."

"I doubt it. When I was up there, Jordan washed his hands of the whole thing. He's been ignoring Marvin's little flaws for years, so now he's swung just as far to the other extreme."

"I'm mighty hungry," said Titus O'Herne.

I got to my feet. "Right you are," I said. To Ron, I said, "I'll be over at Cathy's place for a while. If Crawford manages to get you out tonight, come on over."

"I will," he said.

27

BILL AND CATHY AND I made a glum, silent trio for
dinner. Bill was glum and silent because that was
his natural state, Cathy was glum and silent because
she was still somewhat mad at me on general princi-
ples, and I was glum and silent because I had a hell of
a lot to think about and very little of it was cheery.

Item: Jordan Reed wasn't worried about me going
to the CCG. *Item:* Ron Lascow was in jail on a
trumped-up charge that just might get a conviction if
the political climate was right. *Item:* Jack Wycza had
canceled his deal with me and called in his whole
family. And a lot of them, being duly sworn-in cops,
possessed guns. *Item:* Paul Masetti who seemed to be
as honest as he was unpleasant, had been pulled out
of town by the CCG. *Item:* The guy who'd been
shooting at me was still running around loose.

A dandy series of items. Dinner lay like wet cotton in my stomach, and cigarettes tasted like cardboard.

Hal Ganz called during dessert, saying he'd been looking all over town for me and asking if he could come over. He sounded about as excited and worried as phlegmatic Hal possibly could, so I told him sure, come on over. He arrived at six-thirty, and breathlessly delivered his news. "All the North Side people on the Force have left. All the Wyczas." Trust Hal to be second to bring the news.

"I know," I said.

"They're *police*," he said. He couldn't understand it.

"They're Wyczas," I answered.

We were all together in the living room, Bill Casale quiet in his corner, Cathy and I on the sofa, Hal sitting tense on the edge of an armchair. Cathy now reached over and touched my arm, saying, "How much can you rely on the CCG, Tim?"

"I'm not sure anymore," I admitted. "At first, I thought they were honest. That's the way Masetti looked, anyway."

"But he's gone," said Hal, discovering another piece of news to deliver second. "He left this afternoon."

"There's a new man coming in this evening," I said.

"Why?" he asked, baffled again. "Why should they switch their men around like that?"

"I don't know," I said. "But I'd sure like to find out."

"How can you?" Cathy asked me.

"This is something," I said, reaching for the phone, "that I should have done long ago." And I placed a long-distance call to New York, person-to-person, to Terry Samuelson, the guy who had written the letter of introduction Masetti had given me.

When he came on the line at last, I identified myself and answered two or three questions about how things were going in little old Winston, and then I said, "This guy Paul Masetti got in touch with me yesterday, Terry."

"Oh, yeah," he said. "The letter of recommendation."

"I was wondering just how much of a guarantee that letter was," I said. "You weren't pressured into writing it or anything, were you?"

"Hell, no," he said. "I've known Paul for seven, eight years. He's as honest as they come. I'd recommend him to anybody for anything."

"What about the organization he's with? What do you know about them?"

"The Citizens for Clean Government? Only what Paul told me."

"And what did he tell you?"

"He said they weren't perfect, but they gave him pretty much of a free rein, and it was possible to get a lot of good work done with them."

"But they weren't perfect," I said.

"I got the impression," he said carefully, "that he didn't care for the way the outfit had handled things once or twice, didn't care for a couple of the people connected with it. But it didn't matter to him what the rest of them were like, so long as they let him do things the way he wanted."

"So you don't *know* that the whole organization is honest."

There was silence on the line for a long second, and then he said, in a small voice, "Have I goofed, Tim?"

"I'm not sure," I told him. "Maybe we all have. I'll call you in a day or two."

"Tim, if I've thrown you a curve, I'm sorry, boy, you know I—"

"Sure, Terry, I know. I'll call you in a day or two."

I hung up and looked at the three faces watching me. "Masetti he'll vouch for," I said. "The CCG he can't vouch for."

"And Masetti," said Cathy softly, "is gone."

"In maybe ten minutes," I said, getting to my feet, "I'll find out where the CCG stands in all this."

"Should I come along?" said Bill.

"No. You wait here. I'll be back as soon as I can."

28

DANILE had already arrived at the hotel. I got his room number from Charlie, the desk man, and told him to never mind announcing me, I'd announce myself. Then I took the elevator up and knocked on his door.

The door opened after a minute, and I came face to face with my second example of the Citizens for Clean Government. This one, Archer Danile, turned out to be a huge, full-faced, red-haired, florid individual who looked upon all the world, it seemed, with the same high degree of impersonal contempt. His eyes were small and pale blue, set deep beneath shaggy red brows, and his mouth was a thin wide line, permanently down-curved at the corners. The backs of his fingers were underbrushed with straggly red hairs, and the red-hair motif was followed through in thick waves atop his head. His massive chest and stomach were covered by a broad expanse of white shirt, with a black tie draped precisely down the middle of all the whiteness. He wore a black suit, the jacket open, and on his red-haired left wrist was a watch with a gold band.

"Archer Danile?" I said.

He nodded, slowly and with dignity.

"I'm Tim Smith," I said. "Mr. Masetti may have mentioned me."

"Licensed investigator," he said. It was a category, and I'd just been filed away in it, and that took care of me.

I nodded and stuck out my hand, to see what he'd do with it.

He shook it. His handshake was too strong to be natural, and I got the idea this was a man who constantly tested his fellow beings for the degree to which they had failed to reach perfection, the yardstick being, quite naturally, himself.

I felt somewhat more optimistic. Judging by Masetti, a prerequisite for an honest, unbribable reformer was a miserable personality. Danile seemed to have that qualification to excess.

He frowned, puckering his lips out the way Sidney Greenstreet used to do, and when he said, "Come in," I knew it was only after a long interior struggle.

He turned away into the room, leaving me to close the door after myself. I did so and went down the two-pace-long hall to the living room of the suite. Danile, ahead of me, settled himself down upon the sofa with the weighty dignity of Henry the Eighth at a rural court of high justice, and motioned with one hand for me to take the armchair to his right.

I did so, and he said, "Quite frankly, Mr., uh, Smith, I am not as yet fully apprised of the situation here in Winston. I haven't yet read Mr. Masetti's report, and so I honestly don't know just what the current status is in this city, nor where you stand within it."

"Masetti asked me to co-operate with the CCG," I said. "I turned him down, thinking my loyalty was more to the people in the town than to outsiders."

He nodded heavily. "An attitude, unfortunately, that we quite often have to contend with."

"But there've been a number of changes since then," I went on. "Two people have been murdered in attempts to kill me. I no longer have any feeling of loyalty to stop me."

"And now you do wish to co-operate with us, is that it?"

"That's it."

He pursed his lips again, thinking, his eyes gazing off into the middle distance. At last he said, "And of what would this co-operation consist, Mr. Smith?"

"Information," I told him. "Kickbacks, nepotism, fake construction bids, mismanagement of municipal funds . . ."

"I see." He rested his hands in his lap, and tapped the tips of his fingers together. He studied the effect for a while, and then said, "You have learned of all these things in the time since Mr. Masetti talked to you?"

"No. I have comprehensive files for the last fifteen years."

"Files?" He looked at me. "You mean you have known of these things for fifteen years?"

"I've kept complete files," I said.

"Have you ever, before this, attempted to get this information into the hands of the proper authorities?"

I shook my head. "That wasn't my job. My job was—"

"Not your *job*?" He sounded honestly shocked. "Surely, Mr. Smith, it is every citizen's job—"

"No," I said. For all his individual personality and appearance, completely unlike Masetti, he wound up spouting the same tired civics-class garbage. "My job," I told him, "was to be a confidential investigator. If the facts I learn wind up in court, I'm not useful."

He shook his head slowly back and forth, the lips once more pursed. "I don't know, Mr. Smith," he said. "I have no idea what sort of arrangement Mr. Masetti had in mind, or what offers he made you, if any, but I'm afraid I'll have to know quite a bit more about the situation here in Winston before agreeing to do business with you. If you are attempting now to gain immunity for yourself by making some sort of deal with the Citi—"

"Immunity? What the hell kind of immunity?"

"Now, really, Mr. Smith," he said ponderously. "After all, you *have* just stated to me that you have in your possession a record of governmental crimes in this community covering the last fifteen years, and that you have, until this very moment, never once attempted to reveal this information to the proper authorities. Quite the reverse. You have gone so far as to admit to me that you have actively concealed the evidence of these crimes."

"Never!" This interview wasn't going at all as I'd expected, and I was beginning to lose my temper. "I have never," I told him angrily, "concealed the *evidence* of any crime. The evidence has always been there, and is there now. And any proper authority who's interested can go find it exactly the way I did, by looking for it. It isn't my job to do the *proper authority's* work for it."

"Your job, as you describe it, Mr. Smith," he said pompously, "is a dishonest one."

"As a matter of fact," I went on, talking over him, "what lousy proper authorities anyway? The District Attorney? He's one of the biggest crooks in the state. The Mayor? The Chief of Police?"

"That isn't the point," he said.

"Why the hell isn't it? I *live* in Winston, in the real world. I have to make my living in Winston, in the real world, and that means I have to make my peace with the people who *run* Winston, and who *run* the real world. I tried that, and it's always worked pretty well. Now you people have come in and rattled this town out of its wits, and that arrangement doesn't work anymore. I'm adapting myself to the new conditions, that's all. I'm no more honest or dishonest, in the vague abstract total way you use those terms, than anybody else alive in the world. I have a job, an honest and proper job, licensed by the state of New York and the city of Winston, and I do that job as well as I can. And a part of that job is its confidential nature. My job is confidential in exactly the same way that a lawyer's job or a doctor's job or a psychiatrist's job or even a *priest's* job is confidential. Is a lawyer supposed to report every crime he hears described in his office? Is a priest supposed to report every crime he hears described in the confessional?"

"That is not the same thing, Mr. Smith!" And from the shocked, wide-eyed way in which he said that, I knew I had blasphemed.

"And just why the hell *isn't* it the same thing?" I shouted. I was on my feet now, without knowing how or when I'd stood up, and I kept shaking my fist as I shouted at him. "I've been responsible for crimes solved, reparations made, injustices corrected, *without* the people involved getting into a lot of bad publicity, and without anybody getting a useless jail sentence, and I've—"

"Useless?" That one brought Danile to his feet, too. Blasphemy against the penal system was apparently even worse than blasphemy against the church.

"Yes, you're goddam right, useless! Look, you take a kid—" I had to stop and shake my head and take a deep breath and start all over again, so the words would come out slow enough to be pronounced. "You take a kid," I said. "He burgles a grocery store. The law gets him, and the court gives him six months in a reformatory, and he comes out a worse kid than when he went in. And ten years and four penitentiaries later, he winds up in one of these modern clinks with the pastel-pink bars and more psychiatrists than prisoners, and they spend five years trying to undo the damage that was done by that reformatory."

"That's an oversimplification!" he shouted.

"How *else* are we going to talk, if we don't simplify, you fat-headed fact-filled do-gooder?"

"I didn't come here—"

"To be insulted, I know. All right, now listen. You take that same kid, only instead of the law getting him, I get him. And nobody knows about his crime but me and the grocer and his parents. He gets the scare of his life, when he sees how easily he was caught, and he gets the word on what would have happened if the cops had found him instead of me, and the grocer gets his money back, and the kid never pulls that kind of stunt again."

He shook his head rapidly, saying, "And you accuse *me* of idealism, when you expect—"

"Expect, hell! That's what *happened!* That is exactly what happened with a kid who broke into Joey Casale's grocery store. The hell with your theories. I'm telling you what *works,* and I'm trying to tell you what the goddam *system* is in this world, and how I fit into that system. And if I *don't* fit into that system, I'm *through.*"

"If Satan himself—" he started, but I cut him off. "You're goddam one hundred per cent right!" I snapped. "If Satan himself were Mayor of Winston, and all the lesser devils had all the offices in City Hall, *they would be the ones running my world.* And if I expected to *live* in that world, I would have to make my peace with them."

"Make a deal with them, you mean."

"Say it any way you want," I said.

He took a deep breath, then suddenly turned away from me and walked over to the window. He stood looking down at Winston for a long minute, and then he glanced back at me and said, "You ought to leave Winston for a while, Mr. Smith. You ought to leave right away."

And he was a different man. The voice, the manner of speaking, the words, the expression on his face, all were totally different. In that one split-second, he had gone from Archer Danile, reformer and idealist and prim Puritan, to Archer Danile, practical and realistic human being.

The switch was too fast for me. I was still mad at that other Danile, and so my voice was unnecessarily loud and harsh when I said, "Why should I?"

"There are things here you know nothing about," he said. "You live too close to the surface. You shouldn't judge men on the assumption that they, too, live close to the surface. I sympathize with you and, in a way, I agree with you. And I am giving you friendly advice when I suggest that you leave town for a while, and that you do not leave a forwarding address behind you."

"Speak plainly," I said.

He shook his head, smiling a bit. "I have. I can't speak more plainly."

The telephone rang then, interrupting my question before it got fairly started. Scowling, Danile picked up the receiver, listened a moment, and said, "Five minutes." He listened again, and said, "All right. And what about Miss London? Isn't she back in her room yet? . . . Yes, you do that."

He hung up, looked back at me, and said, "Not tonight, Mr. Smith. Perhaps tomorrow, if you are foolish enough to still be in town, and dependent upon circumstances, of course—perhaps tomorrow we can make some arrangement. In the meantime, good night, Mr. Smith."

I studied him, and I could make no sense out of him. "Good night," I said, and left the apartment.

I rode down in the elevator, thinking glum thoughts, and in the lobby I noticed somebody I knew, a little old man in a black suit and a chauffeur's cap. His name was Tommy O'Connell, and he was sitting over in a corner, apparently waiting for somebody, and his presence answered a number of questions.

But I'll take direct evidence in preference to circumstantial evidence every time, as I'd mentioned to Harcum this afternoon. So I walked over and said, "Hi, Tommy."

"Oh, hi there, Tim," he said. He grinned up at me, so he hadn't been told who he should or shouldn't talk to.

"Danile will be down in a couple of minutes," I said.

He nodded. "I know," he said. "The guy on the desk just called him."

So that was that. I said so long to Jordan Reed's chauffeur and walked out of the hotel.

29

THE LIVING ROOM was crowded when I got back to Cathy's place. Aside from Cathy and Bill Casale and Hal Ganz, there were three new arrivals, the presence of all of whom surprised the hell out of me. One of them was Ron, whom I hadn't expected to see out on bail before tomorrow morning. The second was Art, my former bodyguard courtesy of Jack Wycza, whom I hadn't expected to see ever again. And the third was Councilman Myron Stoneman, one of the seven people to whom I'd made my ultimatum the day before.

Everybody wanted to talk at once, including me, and so everybody jabbered and nobody listened, until finally Ron shouted us all down and said, "One at a time, God damn it, one at a time. Let's get straightened out here. Myron, you first."

Myron nodded at Ron. His heavy, not-very-bright-looking face was dark with controlled anger. "Thanks,

Ron," he said. "You've been training yourself for the legislature, I see."

"Speak your piece, Myron," I said.

Myron turned his scowl to me. "I've always thought it a good idea," he said, "to know what my friends and partners are up to. So I've cultivated a few secretaries and clerks—a bush-league spy system—to let me know what's doing in the world. It's paid off. About an hour ago, I got a call from Jordan Reed's secretary. Reed is selling us out. He's wangled a deal with the CCG, him and Harcum and Watkins."

"A deal?"

"The way I hear it," he said sourly, "Jordan has high hopes of being governor."

So that's what Jordan wanted, as substitute for a son. The whole state. "What about the rest of you?" I asked.

"He's throwing us to the wolves. Dan Wanamaker and Claude Brice and Les Manners and Ron over there and you, Tim. A nice all-star lineup for the scandal."

"So they *could* be bought," said Ron softly.

Myron glanced at him and grinned without humor. "They sure as hell could," he said. "Dan Wanamaker and Claude Brice have already left town. Les Manners is reading his law books. I want to know what you people are planning on doing."

Hal Ganz, his faith in human institutions practically indestructible, said, "Are you *sure* they've got a deal with the CCG? Maybe they're just hoping for one, maybe the CCG doesn't know anything about it."

"The CCG knows plenty about it," I told him. "That's why Masetti was pulled out. He was a legitimately honest reformer". The new man they sent in, Danile, is a politician's politician."

"You talked to him, Tim," said Ron. "What did he have to say?"

"The brushoff," I told him. "He didn't want me or anything I could offer him. When I left, Jordan Reed's chauffeur was waiting to take Danile for his meeting with Reed."

"At the plant," said Myron. "That's where she said they were getting together."

"There are six of us here," said Ron. "Not counting Cathy, of course. Maybe it would be a good idea if we all went over to the plant and had a talk with these people."

"No," said Art.

We all turned and looked at him. I'd practically forgotten he was there. I still didn't know whether Jack Wycza had sent him back, or he'd come on his own hook, sticking to the agreement we'd made.

"Why wouldn't it be a good idea?" Ron asked him.

Art looked at me. "I don't know any of these people, Mr. Smith," he said. "Except Bill Casale, there."

"It's all right," I told him. "We're all in the same leaky boat together." I looked around at the others. "This is Art," I said. "He works for Jack Wycza."

"Worked," he corrected me.

I reeled off the names of the other people present, and then said, "Now. Why wouldn't it be a good idea for us to go down to Reed & King?"

"Because Reed and Jack Wycza have combined," he said.

And everybody started talking again.

This time, I was the one who shouted them all down and said to Art, "What do you mean they've combined?"

"Just what I said. They've teamed up. I guess Reed was afraid you people would make trouble. So he and the rest of his crowd are holed up at his plant, and Jack is going there, too, with a small army. That's the deal. Reed promises to protect Jack from the CCG, and Jack supplies the army to protect Reed from you people."

"I guess," said Myron Stoneman slowly, "Dan and Brice had the right idea after all. Leaving town might be the smartest thing to do, under the circumstances."

"No, God damn it!" I was stuck, and I was getting mad, and there was no place for me to get rid of the anger. "I'm not running away," I said. "I'm going to beat these bastards!"

"How?" said Myron.

I glared at him, and shook my head. I didn't know how.

"An army," said Ron softly, as though he couldn't believe it. "For God's sake, he's got an army."

And then we were silent. We were all involved in this, and we were all discovering that we'd wound up on the short end of a very dirty stick. All except Bill Casale, still sitting silently in a corner and waiting to find out who had killed his grandfather.

Bill Casale! By God, *I* had an army, too!

I jumped to my feet. "Bill," I said. He looked startled at being addressed. "One of seven people," I told him, "killed your grandfather. One of them is Myron Stoneman, right over there. Two have just left town. One is at home, trying to find a loophole in his law books. And the other three are out at the Reed & King plant. Now, it's got to be one of those seven."

"Which one?" he asked me. "Not me, Tim," said Myron.

"Shut up," I said over my shoulder. Back to Bill, I said, "What will you do when I tell you which one it was?"

"I'll call my father," he said, "and tell him."

"And then what?"

"Then the family," he said stolidly, "will go get the guy."

"What if he's one of the three at the plant?" I insisted. "Holed up in there with Jack Wycza's crowd from the North Side to protect him."

"We'll still get him," said Bill calmly.

"Are you sure?"

He nodded. "I know my family," he said.

"What if I just tossed out a name?" I asked him. "What if I said right now that Jordan Reed killed your grandfather?"

"Did he?"

"That isn't the point. What if I *said* he did?"

"You'd have to prove it to my father," he said. "The family isn't here just to do your work for you."

I'd done my work too well. I could remember the good old days, when the Casale family was ready to lynch Ron Lascow on no more say-so than the radio. *Now,* when I needed them, they wanted proof.

"If I prove my case, Bill," I said, "and it turns out he's one of the men in the plant, then your family will go get him. Right?"

He nodded.

Suddenly Art chuckled. "Mr. Smith," he said, "You're a wonder."

"I don't understand," said Hal. He was looking in bewilderment from face to face.

"It's easy," Art told him. "Mr. Smith, here, just re-cruited his own army."

"It might not be one of the three, Tim," said Ron.

Hal Ganz said, "Tim, you can't mean it. That isn't the way to do things, Tim, you've got to let the law—"

"If we let the law," Myron interrupted him, "we'll all be on the inside looking out. Oh, not you, I suppose. You look like one of those clean-nosed types. But *I'll* be jailed, and so will Ron Lascow over there, and so will Tim."

"But for God's sake," cried Hal, "a pitched battle—"

"What other way is there, Hal?" I demanded.

"I can't believe the CCG—" he started.

"Hal, wake up," snapped Ron. "You heard what Tim said when he came back. The guy from the CCG is going off to meet Jordan Reed."

"Jack Wycza wouldn't have mobilized his crowd," said Art, "unless he had a pretty strong guarantee from Reed."

Hal shook his head. "There has to be some other way," he said. "If we could send a plea to the Governor—"

Ron said, "No, Hal. I'm sorry, but the answer is no. Let me tell you some politics. The Governor of this state lives in the capital, Albany. He belongs to one political party, and the city of Albany is controlled by the other political party. The way I understand it, the CCG has a close unofficial connection with the Governor's party, and is building up a reputation on small towns in order to get the local machine in Albany. The Governor would very naturally like to see the capital city of the state run by his own party."

"This has gone beyond politics," said Hal desperately.

"For you, maybe," said Myron. "Not for the politicians."

"A thing like this," said Ron, "doesn't leave politics behind until it reaches court, and sometimes not even then. The decision is going to be made in this town long before anybody gets to court. The ones who go to court, indicted by a grand jury, will be the ones who've already lost."

"I don't see what you're trying to convince him for," said Art. "Don't you have other things to do?"

"I think I should leave," said Hal, getting to his feet.

I nodded. "Maybe you're right."

We waited silently until he left, and then Art said, "When does this army of yours go into action, Mr. Smith?"

"That's the tough part," I said. "I have to find out who's been doing the killing. And if it isn't one of the people in the plant, I don't have an army after all."

"It wasn't me," said Myron. "That's all I can tell you. It wasn't me, and I didn't even know about this CCG business until the morning after that gunman tried to kill you."

"Let's do this the old classical way," said Ron. "The three parts of any murder: motive, method and opportunity."

"All right," I said. "Try it and see where it gets you. Opportunity, to begin with. They all had lots of opportunity. The first attempt was made at one in the morning. Myron, where were you?"

He grinned. "Home in bed."

"That's exactly what the other six would say, too. And the second try was when the guy shot at me from City Hall. And all seven were in City Hall at the time."

"My grandfather was killed at eleven-thirty at night," said Bill.

"Another nighttime job," I said. "Again, everybody's home in bed. And the fourth one was the bomb in my car. It could have been put in there anytime over a twelve-hour period, by anybody in the world. So that takes care of opportunity. What's next?"

"Method," said Ron.

I shrugged. "A hired gunman, a grenade, a gun and a homemade bomb. What can you say about method?"

Art said, "Your killer is pretty shy, you can say that much. He doesn't like to show his face."

"Staying out of sight when something illegal is going on," said Ron blandly, "is instinctive with politicians."

"After the first attempt," I said, "I gave Harcum a profile of the guy we were after, on the basis of method. He hired a professional killer out of New York. That meant he was pretty well-to-do. He shot the professional with a hunting rifle, which probably meant he had a hunting license and goes out after deer every fall. And the gunman wasn't worried about being arrested, so the guy who hired him was probably influential locally. There's your profile, based on method. A rich and influential local citizen who has a hunting rifle."

"And who's been to New York recently," added Cathy.

"That profile fits all seven of us," said Myron. "Including me, unhappily. We're all influential locally, God knows, or at least we were up until today. And we all have hunting licenses and hunting rifles. And we've all been to New York sometime within the last month and a half or two months. And"—he offered us a crooked grin—"we've all made out rather well financially."

"Method on the second try," I said. "A gun. Anybody can have a gun."

"On the third try," said Ron, "a hand grenade. I shouldn't think hand grenades would be that easy to come across." He offered us a sour grin. "Except from the National Guard," he said.

"All seven of us," said Myron, "have almost complete run of City Hall. Including the jail and Police Headquarters, down in the basement. I understand they have a variety of weapons in the armory down there, including some souvenir guns and hand grenades and samurai swords taken from our returning veterans after the Second World War."

"On the fourth try," I said, "a homemade bomb. I don't know which one of them has the knowledge to construct a bomb like that. Anybody else?"

"Jordan Reed has his own chemical plant," said Art.

"That's a thought. But does it mean he knows how to make a bomb?"

"And does he," asked Ron, "have the same free access to City Hall that the others have?"

"I suppose he could get any key he wanted, yes," said Myron.

"So they all had opportunity, and any one of them might have used these methods, though Jordan Reed might be more likely for the bomb in the car."

"That leaves motive," said Ron.

"The coming of the CCG," I said. "Once again, they all fit."

"Wait a second, Tim," said Cathy. "You're not saying that right."

"I'm not saying what right?"

"You're saying," she said earnestly, "that wanting somebody dead is a motive for murder. But that isn't right. You have to know *why* the person wanted that other person dead. *That's* the motive. You have to ask yourself why the coming of the CCG made somebody want to kill you."

"I've been going round and round with that question for two days," I told her.

Ron said, "What about this girl that got killed out at Reed's place? Where does she fit into all this?"

"I don't think she does," I said.

"What girl?" asked Myron.

"Girl named Sherri something-or-other," I told him. "Stacked blonde. You might have seen her hanging around with Harcum lately."

"She's dead?"

"Seems she's an old girlfriend of Marvin Reed's," I said. "I guess Harcum was around just to give her transportation here, and the first chance she got she lit out to see Marvin. And wound up with a hunting knife in her, out in the woods by Reed's house."

Cathy said, "And it looks as though Marvin did it, is that right?"

"Looks that way," I said thoughtfully. "Funny thing," I said. "Jordan washed his hands of the whole thing, as soon as he found out Marvin'd been playing around. And Marv said, 'I'd do anything for you.' To his father, he said that."

"So what? "said Ron.

"This is goofy," I said.

Myron said, "You mean, Jordan killed the girl, and Marvin will take the blame?"

"Something goofier than that," I told him. "Marvin will do anything for his old man. Including kill me, do you think? If a bunch of reformers are coming into town, and he knows his father is worried—"

"Not Marvin," said Cathy. "He might kill that girl, because he was all upset. But he wouldn't coldly plan to kill anybody, and just keep trying time after time."

"Let's forget that thing," said Ron, "and go back to the main issue. We were talking about motive."

"And not getting anywhere," I said.

"Why would this guy want to kill you?" Ron asked rhetorically.

"Maybe," said Cathy thoughtfully, "that's the wrong question."

I looked at her. "What other question is there?"

"I'm not sure," she said. "I don't know if this would help or not, but why not ask yourself what would happen if you were dead?"

"What would happen if I were dead?"

She nodded.

"That's the same question."

"No, it isn't," said Ron suddenly. "Cathy may have something there." He looked urgently at me. "Tim," he said, "what would change, what would be different, if you were dead?"

"Nothing right now," I told him. "Two, three days ago, when this all started— I don't know, the CCG would probably have had to go somewhere else to get its evidence, that's all. I can't think of anything else."

"Your files would still be around," said Ron, "where the CCG could probably have gotten hold of them anyway. So that wouldn't make any difference."

"There must have been some definite result the killer had in mind," said Cathy. "Something that would happen if and when you were to die."

"If we could only—" started Ron, but then it hit me. "Wait a minute!" I shouted, and jumped up from my chair. I pointed at Ron, who blinked at me in total confusion. "You said it!" I shouted at him. "You said it!"

He stared at me open-mouthed. "I said what?"

"Wait," I said. "Just wait." I ran to the phone, dialed, waited, and when Charlie came on I said, "Is Sherri London there?"

"She's dead," he said.

"Thanks," I said, and hung up, grinning.

Cathy said, "What is it, Tim? Do you know who it is?"

Bill, suddenly alert, said, "You've got it, Tim?"

"Call your father," I told him. "Call him right now. I've got it cold."

30

I WAS BACK in the Casale Brothers warehouse, but
this time I was face to face with Mike Casale and
the family. It was a large bare room, a few crates lined
up along one wall, and it was full of Casales. The
whole male population of the family was there, plus
some of the truckers who worked for Mike, plus Ron
and Art and Cathy and Myron Stoneman and me.

I started talking the minute I walked in, giving
them everything that had happened in the last couple
days, so they'd have enough facts to understand my
proof. They listened impatiently, and I got through the
history as quickly as I could. Then I said, "I saw it
when Cathy there asked me what would change if I
were dead. It suddenly occurred to me that my filing
cabinet—or its contents, anyway—would immediately
be impounded as evidence in the case. The killer had
already been approached by the CCG, and asked if he

could supply convictable evidence on the rest of the crowd, on the basis that the CCG would leave him alone and pay him off."

"You mean the CCG asked this guy to kill you?" demanded Ron.

"No. They left it to him to get the stuff any way he could. This was the only way."

"Who is this guy?" demanded Mike Casale.

"Hold on," I told him. "I'll get to it. I don't want to toss a name at you, I want to give you the facts, until you can see it for yourselves. Start with the first murder. A hired gunman from New York. Now, who among the people out at that plant now would have the contacts and the knowledge necessary to go to New York and find a professional killer? Could any of *you* do it?"

"Reed could," said Sal Casale.

"Don't rush it," I told him. "Remember what happened after the gunman missed. The police were called, arrived in a prowl car, and a few minutes later the gunman was shot down. Now, put yourself in the killer's place. You hire somebody to do your killing for you, right? Do you then hang around where he's going to do the job? The hell you do. You stay far, far away from the scene of the crime."

"How come he was there?" Ron asked me.

"How come he knew to *get* there?" I countered. "All right, move on to attempts number three and four. Both times he used explosives."

"Reed can get his hands on explosives," said Sal Casale. "He runs a chemical plant."

"He doesn't make hand grenades in that plant," I told him. "That most likely came out of the police armory at City Hall. Now, who could most easily get a hand grenade from the police armory?"

"Any of us," said Myron Stoneman.

"Who would most likely," I went on, "have sometime in his career picked up the knowledge for putting together a homemade bomb? Who could most readily have cut me out of the burglar-alarm system? Who would be most likely to have a police radio in his home, and hear the call to the prowl car that came to the diner, and *know* his hired gunman had missed? And who would gain possession of my files if I were killed and they were impounded as evidence?"

"Harcum," said Sal Casale softly.

"Some of you may have noticed the blonde Harcum's been squiring around the last few days," I said. "Her name is Sherri London. She was murdered this afternoon, and the new CCG man was trying to get in touch with her tonight, not knowing she was dead. She was the contact between Harcum and the CCG. When it was clear that Harcum couldn't deliver, the CCG switched over and made a deal with Reed. Sherri was on her way to him, and Harcum saw himself on the outside again. He tried to stop her from going to Reed, not knowing that Reed had already made the deal in Albany. She wouldn't stop. He had to kill her, hoping he could pin it on Marvin Reed, hoping it would give him time to get back with the CCG."

"Okay, Tim," said Mike Casale. "You've convinced me. We'll take care of him. You and your friends go on now."

"What? What is this?"

He shook his head. "I know what you were counting on, Tim," he said. "You expected us to go tearing in and clean everything up for you. But we're not going to get ourselves killed off for you or anybody else. It's strictly a personal matter, Harcum and us."

"You won't get to Harcum," I warned him, "without fighting the others."

"From what you say," he said, "they make a habit of selling each other out. If we make the request strong enough, I think they'll give him to us."

Art spoke up, suddenly. "I doubt it," he said.

Mike turned and studied Art. "Is that so?"

"Jack Wycza's thrown in with the rest of them," Art said. "And you don't force Jack to do anything. If you try to take Harcum, Jack will fight you."

Mike looked from Art to me, as though wondering what Art's credentials were, and I said, "Art knows what he's talking about. And if you don't show force, the others won't have any reason to give him up."

Sal Casale came forward to stand beside his brother and glare at us. "If we have to fight," he said, "we'll fight. But it'll be *our* fight. You reach for your own chestnuts, Smith."

If that was the way they wanted it— "All right," I said. "It's your show."

"Tim," said Cathy.

"Come on," I said to her. "Come on. Let Mike and the others decide what to do."

Cathy wanted to stay and argue, and so did Ron, but Myron and Art and I herded them out and down the stairs and out of the building, where I shut off their jabbering and said, "Ron, you take Cathy home. Myron, you get lost too."

"I can help, Tim," said Ron.

"You're right, you can. Here's my car keys. Take Cathy home." I turned away, saying to Art, "You still with me?"

"All the way, Mr. Smith," he said. He was grinning again.

Now Cathy started jabbering, but I ignored her and headed down the street toward the Reed & King plant, three blocks away.

At the corner, Art said, "Where now, Mr. Smith?"

"A phone."

"This way."

We turned off Front Street, to the right, walked a block, and found a bar. At the phone booth in back, I said, "I'm going to dial Reed's private number at the plant. You do the talking. Ask for Jack, tell him who and where you are, but don't mention I'm with you. Tell him you worked your way into my confidence, and I'm now leading the Casale family. Tell him the family knows Harcum killed its patriarch, and is about to march on the plant."

Art's grin broadened, and he said, "Making sure there's a war, huh?"

"Right."

He studied me for a second, grinning, and then shook his head in admiration. "Give me a dime," he said.

31

THE REED & KING PLANT, like Casale Brothers, took up a square block of Front Street. Unlike Casale Brothers, three blocks away, this square was neat and pretty as an architect's model. The building was shaped like a plus sign, a long main building with wings jutting out on each side. It was five stories tall, sand-blasted a near-white, and surrounded by black-top parking lots and neatly mowed bits of lawn. The whole block was encircled by hedges four feet tall, except for the broad sidewalk leading up to the main entrance, and the entrances to the two parking lots.

Across the street from the plant was a row of old tenement buildings, most of them empty, a couple used as warehouses, one down at the corner containing a luncheonette, closed at this time of night. Art and I were waiting in the ground-floor living room of one of the empty ones, sitting by the broken-glassed front windows and watching the street and the plant building across the way.

We'd been waiting fifteen minutes when Art whispered, "Here they come!"

I shifted position, and looked out the paneless window. Three people were coming down this side of the street. Mike Casale and his brother Sal and his son Bill. They were the only ones in sight.

I knew what Mike had in mind. They planned to go in there themselves, just the three of them, to give Jack Wycza no fears about their trying to force entry. Then they would try to convince Reed and the others that it would be safer and easier to turn Harcum over, without causing any trouble or any war.

A fine idea, but it wouldn't work. I'd made sure of that.

The three of them passed the building I was hiding in and walked on. They were going to die. I held the splintery window sill and watched, and waited.

They walked on a ways, until they were directly opposite the main entrance of the sprawling unlit plant building. Then Mike led the way across the street, Bill to his right and Sal to his left.

All at once, my head was halfway out the window, and I was shouting, "Don't!" I couldn't do it, I couldn't gun them down that way.

I got the one word out, and Art was dragging me back inside, one hand clamped over my mouth. And the shots cracked from a ground-floor window in the plant.

They had just reached the opposite curb. Mike toppled backwards off the curb, Sal doubled over and collapsed face-first on the sidewalk, and Bill spun around like a toy pulled by a string. He took two steps along the sidewalk, faltering, and another shot rang out. He fell like a tree.

There was absolute silence on the street.

Beside me, I could hear a slight rustling as Art shifted position. Then his whisper sounded, harsh in my ear, "What the hell were you trying to do?"

I couldn't have explained it to him. Not in a million years.

32

SILENCE for ten minutes. The plant building was dark-windowed and still, waiting. The three bodies lay unmoving on the pavement, half-lit by a streetlight farther to the left. There was no traffic and no pedestrians. Front Street was exclusively commercial property and now, almost one in the morning, the only people around were the combatants.

Silence for ten minutes. And then all hell broke loose.

A sudden roar of truck engines came from the right, and a Casale Brothers truck rumbled into sight, followed by another truck and another and another. The first jumped the curb in front of the main entrance to the plant, crossed the sidewalk, plowed through the hedge, and jolted to a stop a yard from the main entrance. The second and third followed the first, passed it, and halted on the lawn between hedge and building. The fourth tore through the hedge on the other side of the main entrance and stopped just behind the first, as two more trucks raced down from the other direction and into the parking lot to the left of the building.

Men poured from the backs of the trucks, carrying rifles and pistols. Red and white light-flashes spurted at the windows as those inside fired on the attackers, and then the Casales had shot the lock off the front door, and burst through and into the building.

There had been maybe sixty men in the trucks that had stopped at the front of the building. Five of these were now lying on the walk near the front door. The rest had surged inside, and I could hear gunfire and shouts from within the building. To the left, a second skirmish had started in the parking lot, out of sight.

The shooting went on and on, spreading out as the Casales moved deeper into the building. A man— Casale or Wycza, I couldn't tell—suddenly burst out the gaping front doorway and ran for the street. He got halfway before fire flared in the doorway behind him, and he hurtled to his face, skidding on the pavement. Glass shattered in a second-story window, and a body dropped out, twisting in the air, crashing onto the hood of one of the trucks.

Then a group of men raced out of the empty building to the left of the one we were in. They dashed directly across the street and through the main entrance of the plant.

Art grunted, and said, "That's Jack. That's his way. Let them into the building, then hit them from two sides." He got to his feet suddenly and said, "If we're going to move at all, Mr. Smith, now's the time."

I kept watching. Mike and Sal and Bill still lay on the sidewalk, out where I could get a good view of them. One of the trucks had driven over Bill's legs. That seemed like a hell of a thing to do.

"Now, Mr. Smith," said Art coldly.

I looked up at him. He didn't think as much of me anymore, and he wasn't bothering to hide it. It must be nice, I thought, to not give a damn. But of course he didn't know any of the Casales. "All right," I said. "Now."

I stood beside him, looking out the window, trying to think. "We'll want to go through the parking lot," I said. "Reed's offices are on that side, on the fifth floor."

"All right," he said.

"We'll go out the back way," I said, trying to think. I closed my eyes. "We'll go down through the back yards to the corner, and cross there."

"All right," he said again. He started away, turned to look at me. "Come on, Mr. Smith," he said.

I opened my eyes. They were still lying there. "All right," I said.

33

THERE WERE maybe a dozen cars scattered around the parking lot, plus the two Casale Brothers trucks. On this side, light shone from windows on the fourth and fifth floors, and I caught occasional glimpses of people moving around inside. There was no one in the parking lot at all.

Art and I were crouched behind the hedge, next to the parking-lot entrance. I whispered, "We'll make a run for that first car, the Dodge. We'll work our way from car to car till we reach the building."

"Lead on, Mr. Smith," he said scornfully. "I'm right in front of you."

I moved out from the hedge and started running, crouched over, weaving as I ran, a stocky idiot who'd lost the reins. Halfway to the Dodge, the ground suddenly shook beneath my feet, and I lost my balance and fell headlong, my pistol flying out of my hand. I landed hard, on the right shoulder, and rolled up against a rear wheel of the Dodge. I sat up fast, spied the revolver lying on the blacktop a few feet off, and lunged for it as the ground trembled again, and this time I heard the sound of the explosion.

Art cried out, and I looked up. The Reed & King building seemed to be framed by a yellow-white halo, and the roar of the explosion tumbled down around me. The halo suddenly expanded, flashing red-white, the ground shivered again, and the thunder of the third explosion drowned out the noises from inside the building. There were two more explosions, and then sudden silence, and at last I managed to scrabble across the blacktop and get the revolver back into my hand.

The silence lasted only a few seconds, and then ragged shooting began again. I struggled to my feet and was about to move forward when someone clutched at my arm, crying, "Tim! Tim! Please, for the love of God!"

I spun around, pulling away from the hand, and stared into the frightened eyes of Marvin Reed. "My father's in there!" he screamed at me. "What's happening? For the love of God, what's happening?"

"What the hell do you care?" I shouted. "He doesn't give a damn about you."

Art was beside me, still unexcited, still giving me his harsh and bitter grin. "Come on, Mr. Smith," he said.

"We've got to help him!" Marvin was crying. "Tim, help me, we've got to get him out of there!"

"Go away, Marvin, go away." He was pawing at me, and I pushed him away, shouting, "I'm not going to help your father, you damn fool! I'm on the other side!"

He stared at me, white-faced, and suddenly his hand was reaching into his coat pocket and coming out again with a gun, and he was screaming something at me. I gaped at him, the gun came up, and the sound of the shot was the loudest thing in the world.

Marvin slammed backwards onto the blacktop, and Art said, "You're going to have to do better than that, Mr. Smith."

My mind just wouldn't work. I stared down at Marvin and I said, "What? What?"

"He didn't shoot you, Mr. Smith," said Art dryly. "I shot him."

A sudden, louder burst of gunfire tore me back to reality. I looked around, and saw that a door in the side of the building was open, and four men were racing across the parking lot. Other men appeared in the doorway, firing after them, and one of the four staggered and dropped. The other three reached a car, scrambled into it, and the car leaped forward, turning sharply to come about and head for the street. The men in the doorway kept firing, and the car tore out of the parking lot, straight across the street, and crashed into the plate-glass window of the luncheonette.

I ducked behind the Dodge and watched. The second group ran across the parking lot. I recognized them as Casales, and then I saw Danile clamber drunkenly from the wrecked car and stand weaving, his hands out in supplication as he mouthed words that were drowned by all the rest of the noise in the world. Suddenly he fell to his knees, his hands still out and his mouth still moving, and toppled forward onto his face.

The Casales reached the car and dragged out the other two. One was a Wycza, and the other was our District Attorney, George Watkins, his round face white with shock.

Art nudged my arm. "What now, Mr. Smith?"

"Through that door," I said. "That leads up to Reed's suite."

"Okay," he said. "Come on."

He ran for the doorway and I chugged after him, expecting any second a bullet from one of the windows to tear into me. But we reached the doorway, dashed into the building, and found ourselves in a stairwell by Jordan Reed's private elevator. A distorted figure lay sprawled face-down on the stairs.

We moved up the stairs, quickly and cautiously. A fire door was closed on the second floor, and we could hear shooting from the other side of it. We kept on going, and ran into a barricade on the third floor. Office furniture was piled across the doorway from the stairwell to the hall. Four Wyczas were behind this barrier, firing spasmodically at someone we couldn't see.

Art and I stood on the landing below, just out of sight of the defenders. Art whispered, "Are you going to use that gun, Mr. Smith?"

"Reed surprised me," I said. "Don't worry, I'll use it."

"You'd better. I won't be able to get all four of them myself."

"I'll shoot, God damn it!"

"All right. I'll take the two on the left." He hesitated, said, "Now!" and jumped out on the landing.

It only took a second. We leaped out where we could see them, and we each fired twice, and they slumped down over their barricade.

It wasn't real. I pointed, and made a noise, and they slumped, not breathing. It wasn't real.

And then it was.

We ran up the stairs, past the barricade, and up the next two flights to the fifth floor. The door here led to Reed's outer office. Art reached for the doorknob and I pulled him away. "Don't be stupid."

He looked at me, studying my face, and suddenly grinned. "You're back, huh?"

"I'm back." And I was. From the minute the three Casales had been gunned down, I'd been out of it, fuzzy and bewildered and afraid. Shooting the two at the barricade had torn me back. I'd had to make a decision there, fast. If I wanted Harcum, I had to get by the men at the barricade. If I wanted him badly enough, all of this was justified and necessary.

I wanted him that badly.

"Right you are, Mr. Smith."

We took our positions, and I reached out, turned the knob, and shoved the door open wide.

Shots rattled from inside, and four holes appeared in the wall opposite the doorway. The shots stopped, and I spun around into the doorway, firing before I saw what I was firing at. Pete and Gar Wycza, both still in their police uniforms, crumpled behind the secretary's desk. Art rushed past me, around the desk, and fired once.

I moved across to the next door, glancing at the men on the floor. Gar Wycza's mouth and eyes were open, and he looked as though he were grinning. I remembered passing him, day after day, up at the corner of State and DeWitt. I remembered him saying, "Good day for drinkin."

The next door led to Reed's office. We worked the same routine again, and this time Art moved first. There were no shots when I pushed the door open. Art hesitated, and then jumped into the doorway, snapping off one shot as he moved. He stopped, looking into the room, and cautiously crossed the threshold. Then he looked back at me, grinning in embarrassment. "Nobody here."

We crossed Reed's office to the next door. Art said, "Where does this one lead?"

"Conference room. We'll change tactics this time. You keep to the side again, but this time you open the door."

"Where you going to be?"

"Right here," I said. I lay down on my stomach, facing the door, the .32 held up in front of me, my elbows on the floor.

Art got into position. "Say when."

"Now."

He pushed the door open, and a Wycza fired two shots over my head. The conference table was tipped on its side, and he was crouched behind it, only his head and one arm showing. He got the two shots off, both high, and then I fired, and he fell backward out of sight.

Art dashed into the room, vaulted over the table, and another defender appeared, scrabbling to his feet, unarmed, backing away, his face a study in pure terror. He managed to say, "Don't," before Art shot him.

I got up from the floor and ran into the room. There were two more doors here, one leading to the dining room and one to Reed's living quarters. They would be in the living quarters. I turned that way just as the door opened and Jack Wycza started in. He stopped short, gaping at me, and then he saw Art. "You dirty louse!" he cried, and his hand came up with a pistol in it.

The three of us all fired at the same time. Jack crashed backward out of the doorway, landing heavily. He half-rolled over, trying to sit up, then fell back and lay still.

"Come on!" I shouted, and ran forward. At the doorway, I paused and looked back. Art was sprawled on the floor, behind the conference table, lying on his left side. Wycza's shot had caught him in the face.

I turned away, stepped over Wycza's body, and suddenly realized I only had two rounds left in my gun. I went back and scooped up Wycza's, a .45 automatic, and checked the clip. The shot he'd fired at Art had been his first. There were seven bullets left. I pushed the clip back into the butt and went on.

I moved cautiously into the next room beyond, which was Jordan Reed's smaller, private dining room. It was empty, and there was only one room beyond it, Reed's bedroom. I started across the dining room, and then I noticed a door open to my right. It led to another flight of stairs. I turned that way, and a slight noise behind me made me spin around, to see Reed in the doorway of the room I'd just come from, a pistol in his hand.

We just stared at each other for a second, and then I said, "Hiya, governor."

I saw his face tighten, the way Tarker's had at the diner. He fired twice as I threw myself to the side and tried to bring Wycza's .45 to bear on him. I hit the floor rolling, came to a stop on my back, and pulled the trigger three times before Reed was flung off his feet and slammed to the floor. A .45 has a lot more power than a .32.

I started to get to my feet, but my left arm wouldn't take any weight. It crumpled under me, and I looked at it and saw the hole in my shirt where a bullet had gone through. The arm didn't hurt at all, but it just wouldn't work right.

I crawled to the wall, climbed up it until I was standing, and turned again to the stairway. Far below me, I could hear the sound of someone clattering down the stairs. I followed, three steps at a time.

This was Reed's personal stairway, with exits only on the fifth floor and at street-level, where it led to the spot where he kept his Lincoln Continental.

I was at the third-floor landing when another explosion rocked the building, and I almost lost my balance and fell down the next flight. I crashed into the wall instead, driving my weight against the left arm. That hurt it.

I bit my lip to make the fuzziness go away, and kept moving. Ahead of me, there was gunfire, a lot of it. I came to the last landing before street-level, and saw three men in police uniform firing out at somebody in the parking lot. There was a fourth guy there, too, behind the cops. He turned to look up at me as I reached the landing. Harcum.

I fired at him, but missed, and he shoved one of the cops ahead of him through the doorway. I saw the cop fall, and Harcum leap over him and out of sight. The other two cops ran out after him.

I went down the last flight like a mountain goat, twisted my ankle at the bottom, and brought up hard against the wall. I looked through the doorway and saw the Lincoln moving jerkily across the parking lot, four Casales running after it and shooting. I ran out, limping, and saw a Casale Brothers truck off to my left. I hobbled to it and climbed into the cab. As I'd hoped, the driver had been in too much of a hurry to take the keys with him. I started the engine, swung the truck around, and took off after the Lincoln. The windshield spattered in front of my face and I crouched down behind the wheel, just barely looking out over the hood.

The Lincoln reached the street, wobbling badly from two flat tires, and swung right. But the driver couldn't control it anymore, and it veered back to the left again. I pulled up on the right, swung the wheel hard, and drove the Lincoln up over the curb and into the stoop of one of the empty buildings.

I clambered down from the cab, my bad ankle not wanting to support my weight, and fell against the trunk of the Lincoln. They were piling out, and I fired through the back window, hitting one of the cops. The other one was apparently already dead. And Harcum was out and running, fat but agile, diving through a shattered basement window and out of sight.

To have followed him that way, I would have had to silhouette myself in the window, the streetlight behind me. Instead, I climbed up onto the Lincoln, the .45 tucked under my belt because I only had my right arm to work with, and crawled through a first-floor window into the living room. I got the .45 into my hand again and limped cautiously across the room, the floor scattered with brittle lengths of ancient wallpaper. I moved slowly, trying not to make any noise, and finally got out to the hall. I found the door leading to the basement and waited, leaning against the wall.

A couple of minutes went by. Outside, I could hear the muffled sounds of the battle still raging. In the distance, coming steadily closer, the wail of fire engines. Looking up, I saw through the doorless front entrance an angry red glow. The plant was burning.

My mind kept wanting to think about tomorrow, but it couldn't. Harcum was in this building, and my arm was beginning to throb. There wasn't any such thing as a tomorrow anyway.

Another explosion bellowed out from the plant, drowning out the roar of the fighting.

I waited, thinking, *Get it over with, Harcum, come up here and get it over with. You and the others, you've ripped everything to pieces, and I've helped, and now let's finish it.*

The basement door slowly opened, and a darker shadow came out to the shadowy hallway, silhouetting itself against the red glow in the entrance. Round, plain Harcum, who had tried four times to kill me and not shown himself to me once.

He crept slowly down the hallway toward the front of the building, and I could make out the gun he was holding tensely in his right hand. I stood away from the wall, the .45 trained on his round figure, and I said, "Face me, Harcum. For once in your life, face me."

But he wouldn't. The second I started to talk, he ran. I cried, "Harcum!" but he kept running, through the doorless entrance and outside, above the crushed stoop and the wrecked Lincoln. He was framed there for a second, against a double-glow of yellow street-light and angry red from the flaming plant, and then a ragged volley of shots tore and jerked him like a marionette, till the strings were suddenly clipped and he plummeted off the broken stoop and out of sight.

I hadn't killed him. I had come to kill him, I had emptied two guns, I had caused all this waste, and it had taken someone else to kill Harcum. He wouldn't face me.

I limped forward, and was almost to the door when the big explosion came, shaking the building like a gambler shaking a dice cup, and I staggered, putting my weight on the bad leg. I fell, losing the gun, and lay on my face, waiting for the trembling of the building to lessen and stop. It did, finally, and I struggled back to my feet.

Outside, the fire engines were arriving, their sirens screaming down through the octaves to a dying-away guttural groan. There were no more shots, only the shouting of the survivors and the incredibly loud crackling of flames.

I moved along the wall to the front entrance and peered out. The plant was wrapped in flames, fantastically tall and loud and bright, and in their glare I could see the firemen hurrying about their business, and the police cars arriving, bearing the neutral cops, the Hal Ganz kind of cop.

It was difficult to climb down the pile of lumber that had once been the front stoop. I had to crawl down backwards, and when I reached the bottom I heard Cathy calling my name, over and over again, from far, far away.

I turned around, and Cathy was way down the street, running toward me. But between us was a Casale, standing directly in front of me, cradling a shotgun.

He looked at me, icy cold. "You set this up, you son of a bitch," he said. "You set this up."

I whispered, "I had to."

He raised the shotgun.

The sound I heard was Cathy screaming.

About the Author

One of the most prolific popular authors of the twentieth century, Donald Edwin Westlake got his start in pulp fiction, writing under several different pen names in a variety of genres. Author of over one hundred books, he was an Academy Award nominee and three-time Edgar Award winner, having garnered that honor in three different categories. Born in Brooklyn and raised in Albany, Westlake died while on vacation in Mexico on New Year's Eve, 2008.

To see our other great titles,
visit us at:

BLACKBIRD BOOKS
www.bbirdbooks.com